THE RUNNING FLAME

WEATHERHEAD BOOKS ON ASIA

WEATHERHEAD BOOKS ON ASIA

WEATHERHEAD EAST ASIAN INSTITUTE, COLUMBIA UNIVERSITY

For a complete list of books in the series, please see the Columbia University Press website.

THE RUNNING FLAME

A NOVEL

FANG FANG

TRANSLATED BY

MICHAEL BERRY

Columbia University Press   *New York*

This publication has been supported by the Richard W.
Weatherhead Publication Fund of the Weatherhead
East Asian Institute, Columbia University.

Columbia University Press wishes to express its appreciation for
assistance given by the Pushkin Fund in the publication of this book.

Columbia University Press
Publishers Since 1893
New York   Chichester, West Sussex
cup.columbia.edu

Cataloging-in-Publication Data available from the
Library of Congress
ISBN 978-0-231-21500-8 (hardback)
ISBN 978-0-231-21501-5 (trade paperback)
ISBN 978-0-231-56057-3 (ebook)
LCCN 2024050145

Printed in the United States of America

Cover design: Chang Jae Lee
Cover image: Shutterstock

CONTENTS

THE RUNNING FLAME

I

Yingzhi wondered what she should say.

She was sitting with her back against the wall. The wall was sullied with layers of multicolored stains. This dirty wall was where she directed her gaze when she was trying to forget all the horrific things she had experienced. She would try to figure out what each of those stains was. She wondered who was the first person to have left their mark on that wall. Was it just a mark left there by accident, or was it the result of someone letting out their emotions? But one thing was for certain: no one who spent an extended period of time in this room could have ever been in a very good mood.

At that moment she saw a line of dark red characters written on the wall directly facing her. They were written in blood. The characters were crooked and sloppy; each one looked like a stick figure whose limbs had been detached. The characters read, *Why don't you love me?*

Yingzhi sighed as she thought, *Whoever wrote that was hopelessly in love. If she really did die for love, it was probably worth it. It meant that for at least one moment in her life she had experienced true happiness . . . but what about me?*

Sister Yu was asleep in the bed beside Yingzhi. She had once told Yingzhi that those words were written by a woman named Fenping. Over the course of their five-year relationship, Fenping's boyfriend had forced her into getting four abortions, and then one day he nonchalantly told her that he had never really loved her. In the grip of anger, Fenping poisoned his food. Her boyfriend's face turned a pale blue as he died. Fenping spent five months here before they executed her. It was spring when they took her out to be shot. That day everyone in the cell was saying that the flowers outside must be in full bloom. Fenping thought so too. She even talked about how much she loved the touch-me-not flowers growing behind their courtyard wall. That's when they came to take her away. Everyone knew she was never coming back.

High up on the wall, just below the ceiling, was a window. During the daytime that window was always a dull gray color, almost as if someone had taped a piece of paper over the window. Yingzhi couldn't remember ever having seen any trace of sunlight pass through that window. She wondered if her eyes had lost the ability to even perceive sunlight.

Each and every night, Yingzhi felt as if there were a flame chasing her. The running flame would race toward her, its raging fires licking the sky. When the wind would blow, the flames would collapse in one direction. As that flaming tongue pulsated, it resembled a gaping bloodthirsty mouth waiting to be fed. It emitted all kinds of strange and horrible cries, which echoed through the surrounding wilderness.

Sister Yu said it was just a nightmare. Everyone here has nightmares, terrible nightmares.

But Yingzhi knew that wasn't entirely true.

Let me start over again, Yingzhi said.

As she began to speak, the tears rushed down Yingzhi's face. Being able to tell her own story was as painful as being cut with a knife. But Yingzhi knew she had to get this out. She knew that if she didn't say her piece, that flame would never be extinguished; even after death, it would continue raging . . .

II

I t began in autumn.

For a country girl like Yingzhi, all year round the days tended to be rather quiet and uneventful. That was the year she graduated from high school, but Yingzhi didn't get into college. There was nothing terribly attractive for Yingzhi about going to college; anyway, what was the point of spending all that money to go to school? Yingzhi's two classmates who came from the same village also didn't go to college: Chunhui had damaged her vision from too much reading, and Yonggen was basically an idiot. Yingzhi would often help them out when it came to basic tasks. For instance, she would always hold Chunhui's hand when they walked together; or whenever Yonggen's chain came off his bike, he would ask Yingzhi to fix it for him. Yingzhi always felt thankful that she was so much better off than they were. So the fact that she didn't get into college didn't depress her in the least. Once she left high school behind, she knew that she would never again set foot in another school. That was a big relief for her. She actually never wanted to go to college.

Yingzhi grew up in a village called Phoenix Dike. It was only around a dozen *li* from the county seat. She knew that everyone said that people from Phoenix Dike were particularly shrewd and bright. But that shrewdness never seemed to be much help when it came to pulling Phoenix Dike out of its poverty. Ying-zhi's family circumstances were considered above average when compared with those of the rest of the village. Although Ying-zhi's father worked in the fields, her mother ran a small shop beside the road near the village entrance where she sold basic everyday necessities like fuel, rice, oil, and salt. That meant that they were much better off than those families who had to rely exclusively on farming. Except for the wealthiest families in Phoenix Dike, it was hard to think of many others in the village who were doing as well as Yingzhi's family.

Ever since she was little, Yingzhi had heard the stories about how all the shrewdness reserved for the village of Phoenix Dike ended up concentrated in one person—Sanhuo. When Sanhuo went to school, he made it into one of the best schools in the county seat. When Sanhuo was a Red Guard, all he had to do was snap his fingers and people would follow him wherever he went—they even followed him all the way to Hankou. When-ever Sanhuo had a new idea, he always knew how to turn it into money. And that's how it always went with him. During the winter months when there wasn't much to do in the vil-lage, one of the villagers' favorite pastimes was to gossip about Sanhuo. Sanhuo's father was a singer, and people from miles around hired him to sing at their weddings and funerals. He would sing local opera for weddings and celebratory events and mournful songs at the funerals. Even in tough times, their family always managed to do pretty well. Once Sanhuo's father died, there was no one else left to look after the family, so San-huo stepped up to become the head of household. He carried on his father's job as a singer. Of course, his voice couldn't measure up to his father's, but no one seemed to care. Sanhuo even formed his own troupe, which he called the Sanhuo Band.

Everyone knew that if they needed music for some occasion, all they had to do was hire the Sanhuo Band. Whenever they had a job, Sanhuo would ride around the village on his bicycle calling out for his band; it didn't take long for him to assemble the whole crew, which included a *suona* player, a drummer, an *erhu* player, and someone on the clapper. Sanhuo himself couldn't play a note, keep a beat, or hold a tune—all he did was put the troupe together. But Sanhuo was quite the talker, and he was always willing to take on a job; in the end, his troupe was even better known than his father's. Sanhuo was the first person in the village to build his own brick house. It had a red tile roof and white walls; in the middle of the main room was an electric light that hung from the ceiling—when that light turned on each night, people's faces lit up and the eyes of practically everyone in the village turned red with jealousy. Sanhuo had a talent for being able to make money regardless of what changes were going on in society.

Yingzhi had two brothers who wanted nothing more than to be just like Sanhuo. Both of them went from Guangzhou to Manchuria working their skin to the bones, but when they returned home, they were just as dirt poor as the day they left. One of them even contracted a venereal disease. Sanhuo laughed his ass off at them; the sound of his laughter was like the whistling wind whizzing over your head. He laughed so hard that everyone thought he must have laughed his guts out. It was against the backdrop of Sanhuo's laughter that Yingzhi's poor brothers dragged themselves back to their old haunt—the mah-jongg table. Sanhuo commented, "People who gamble better not ever think of getting a real job. People who have a real job better never think about gambling. It all comes down to a question of fate. Sometimes even if you want to change, it turns out to be much more difficult than you can ever imagine."

Sanhuo was already nearly forty-eight years old. His skin was as old and coarse as Yingzhi's father's. Yingzhi's father was almost ten years older than Sanhuo. Sanhuo pointed to his face and said, "Scientists say that people with a lot of grooves in their brains are smarter. I've got so many grooves in my brain that now they are starting to show on my face!" Sanhuo was always jokingly bragging about himself like that. He started getting on Yingzhi's nerves when she was only three years old; all these years later she still despised him.

But Sanhuo never seemed to notice how much Yingzhi was annoyed by him. And the day after she graduated high school, Sanhuo showed up at her door looking for Yingzhi.

Yingzhi was outside in their courtyard playing poker with her nephew, Shaoya. Sanhuo called out, "Yingzhi, you're back?"

Yingzhi didn't bother looking up and instead just mumbled "uh" before turning to Shaoya to warn him, "Don't you dare cheat."

Sanhuo asked, "Hey Yingzhi, what's the fun of that? You can't even win any real money!"

Yingzhi rolled her eyes. "I'm not trying to win any money! My parents can take care of me just fine!"

Sanhuo snickered. "Will they take care of you until you're old?"

Yingzhi didn't bother responding to that question, but she knew he was right; her parents weren't going to live forever.

Shaoya said, "What's it to you? My aunt likes to play cards. You got a problem with that?"

Sanhuo responded, "Supposing there was an opportunity to bring in some cash, ask your aunt if she would rather play cards or make some money?"

Yingzhi could feel her heart racing. Did she really need to answer that question? After all, who wouldn't want to make some money? But because Yingzhi always found Sanhuo so revolting, she refused to answer him. Instead she just turned to

Shaoya. "It's your turn. And let's cut the bullshit and just focus on our game."

"So you don't want to earn some cash?" pushed Sanhuo.

"How could such a great opportunity like that ever fall into my lap?" Yingzhi sarcastically replied.

"And what if it did?" asked Sanhuo.

That's when Yingzhi raised her voice and declared, "Then why wouldn't I take it?"

Those words were music to Sanhuo's ears; he gleefully laughed, and the sound of his laughter was like a saw. Yingzhi couldn't help giving him a piece of her mind: "If you want to gloat, go somewhere else! Just the sound of your laughter gives me a headache!"

"Okay, okay, okay," responded Sanhuo. "Then why don't I tell you something that will be sure to cure your headache."

Sanhuo went on to explain his plan: These days there is no one in the countryside around here who is interested in traditional opera anymore for their weddings and funerals. The times have changed, and there is no market for the old stuff. Everyone today wants to hear pop songs—they're especially taken with those songs from Hong Kong and Taiwan. As soon as the audience hears those tunes, they all start to nod their heads to the beat. Everyone loves the stuff. So he replaced everyone in his Sanhuo Band with new members. He also invested in a karaoke machine and a loudspeaker system, and he hired a bunch of young people as singers. Last month he brought his new troupe to Liujia Marsh. No one could have imagined that as soon as they set up their stage there and struck up the music, a continuous stream of people would keep coming in to listen. They ended up putting on a string of shows that were all warmly received. The audience couldn't stop requesting songs. Eventually there were even people from the other side of the river who paddled over on boats to get in on the excitement. Next month the results of the college entrance exams will be announced, and there are bound to be all kinds of celebrations for those kids going off to college. A few families already booked him for their parties. The current rate is 500 yuan for a single event. When things get busy he can raise the price to 600. There is an extra charge for requesting songs; each singer can make a good haul from each show.

Yingzhi sat there listening. After taking it all in, she thought it sounded like a good business venture. But she didn't want to seem too desperate. "Since you already hired a new band, what do you need me for?"

"I do have three guys I hired; one of them is the DJ and the other two sing. So we are all set in that department," Sanhuo explained. "But I've got only one girl in the troupe, which isn't enough for my audience. I know you have a good voice. I once heard you sing the song '99 Roses' during a Spring Festival celebration; you sounded great. So what do you say? Want to join our band?"

Deep down Yingzhi was secretly ecstatic. She always loved singing. If she was really able to sing like a pop star and make money while doing it, wouldn't that be amazing? But Yingzhi nonetheless insisted on putting up a front. "You're just messing with me," she answered.

But Sanhuo insisted, "Why would I joke about this? We've even got a show this afternoon. I can pay you today if you show up! If you still don't believe me, come by and see for yourself. If I don't pay you, I'll run three laps around your house as punishment!"

By this time it seemed clear that Sanhuo wasn't joking. Yingzhi quickly agreed. "Okay then, I'll be there."

Before he left, Sanhuo gave Yingzhi all the details about when and where to meet. As soon as Sanhuo was out of sight, Yingzhi took those playing cards and tossed them into the air. The cards fluttered through the air and landed all over the ground. Shaoya was so pissed that that he mockingly cursed his aunt as he picked up the cards: "I'll sing, all right! I'll sing you to your grave! You just messed up a perfectly good deck!"

"Are you putting a curse on me?" Yingzhi jokingly protested. "Well, after I'm dead I'll come back as a ghost to tear off that dirty mouth of yours!"

As she spoke, Yingzhi ran into the house to pick out what to wear. Yingzhi had only a few outfits; she had a few things she used to wear to school but nothing suitable to wear on stage. When she couldn't find anything, she rushed into the kitchen to complain to her mother. Yingzhi said that no matter how poor they might be, they should at least have enough money to buy their daughter a proper outfit. Yingzhi was their only daughter and had long grown accustomed to whining to her mother to get her way. Her mother retorted by saying that every article of Yingzhi's clothing was nicer than her own; why weren't they good enough for her to wear? Yingzhi said she didn't have a single pretty dress. Hearing them arguing, Yingzhi's aunt dug out a dress she used to wear when she was younger and gave it to Yingzhi. She said it no longer fit her anyway, so she gave it to Yingzhi. Her aunt's dress was light red and adorned with scattered yellow floral patterns. It had a sharp collar, and on the back were two ribbons that formed a butterfly pattern. Although it was a bit old, the dress looked very pretty once Yingzhi put it on.

Sanhuo's eyes lit up as soon as he saw Yingzhi in that outfit. He applauded. "Good job! You'll do even better if you dress up like that."

Their show was held at Old Temple Village, which got its name from the old temple just beyond the village. Old Temple Village was around forty *li* away from Phoenix Dike. The event was a wedding celebration for the son of the village chief, who even sent a car to pick up the members of the Sanhuo Band. While in the car, Sanhuo handed Yingzhi a list of the songs and asked her which ones she knew how to sing. Yingzhi took a quick look and said that she knew almost all of them. There were a few clothing stores near her school gate that used to blast those songs all day long. Sanhuo encouraged her to pick out her favorite songs from the list to sing. Yingzhi selected "Raining Heart," "The Full Moon," "1,000 Paper Cranes," "Visit Home Often," and finally "99 Roses." Sanhuo got excited and insisted that no matter what, she had to sing "99 Roses." All those were songs that Yingzhi knew like the back of her hand. The guy working for Sanhuo as a DJ was called Wentang. Wentang said that they should do a short practice run before the concert to make sure she could keep up with the rhythm.

The village chief lived in a three-story brick house; the wall facing the main road was lined with yellow ceramic tile. It was an even more impressive than Sanhuo's house. Even from a distance it was quite an eye-catching structure. Sanhuo explained that the village chief was like the emperor in this village—that's why he used the imperial color of yellow. Sanhuo had traveled widely around all the local villages, so what he said seemed to make sense.

The troupe set up their stage right under the window of the eastern wing of the village chief's house; it was a decent distance from the main entrance to the house. The stage was about the size of two beds and was raised about a meter and a half off the ground, making it pretty easy to get on and off it. Sanhuo had personally designed the stage. It was constructed from several sheets of plywood affixed to a wooden frame. All together there were eight sections, which made it very convenient to assemble and disassemble. Once the stage went up, they would cover the surface with a red acrylic carpet; it was an old carpet and who knows who gave it to Sanhuo. Two speakers were set up right in front of the stage. The microphone at center stage looked proper and formal just like the kind political leaders used to deliver official addresses. Once they set up the stage, hooked up the electricity, and started the music, crowds of people immediately began congregating around the stage.

The whole thing came as a surprise to Yingzhi. The feelings of repulsion she had for Sanhuo also seemed to change. Yingzhi even told Sanhuo that she never imagined just how good the production was. Sanhuo responded by telling her, "I'm not trying to brag, but for hundreds of miles around, my troupe is known as the very best one out there! This is how we run things. The people who book us for events are expecting this level of quality. So I have to make sure I give them what they ask for. That's how you keep them happy; otherwise, who would hire us?"

Yingzhi realized that Sanhuo had quite a system worked out.

Whenever people held weddings, crowds of guests would come and go, but all the Sanhuo Band had to worry about was making sure the songs kept going. Their speakers were so loud that the music could be heard from one side of the village to the other, and if you stood too close, you might even damage your eardrums. Some of the audience members would request songs and others would bring bouquets of flowers up to the stage; the whole thing was quite entertaining. The first time Yingzhi went on stage, she wasn't at all nervous; it was actually quite exciting, almost euphoric. With that euphoria, her performance was able to reach a new level of inspiration. Yingzhi felt that she had never sung so well in her entire life. At the end of her first song, the audience broke out in thunderous applause. At that point the bride hadn't yet arrived and the guests were all chatting and laughing; everyone seemed quite happy, and they were all requesting songs to dedicate to various people. Every time they announced who the next song was dedicated to, the crowd would explode in another wave of laughter. All the laughter made the village chief extremely pleased. He immediately slipped all the singers 10 yuan tips. Sanhuo leaned over to tell Yingzhi that half of that tip money was his—that was the rule.

The village chief's son had a lot of friends. They all kept dedicating songs to each other. They talked, laughed, got in a few squabbles, and a few of them even yelled at each other; in the end, the ground was covered with cigarette butts and the whole scene was quite lively. After singing song after song, they insisted that some tall guy go up to the stage to belt one out. As they pushed him up on stage, they insisted that he sing a duet with the girl wearing the floral-patterned dress. The tall guy resisted and kept refusing to sing. Everyone in the audience broke out in laughter at the ridiculous scene. Then a fat man with dark skin yelled, "Guiqing, if you sing, I'll let you off the hook for all the money you lost last night!" Another man with a bald head added, "That's right, just one song and I'll forgive that debt you owe me!"

The tall guy named Guiqing stopped resisting. "Do I have your word?"

The bald man said, "I hereby swear that if I'm lying, I will meet a terrible death!"

The fat man added, "If I'm lying, I'll be admitting I'm the biggest son of a bitch!"

Guiqing laughed. "Okay then, Baldy will die a terrible death and Fatty will be the biggest son of a bitch!"

Before Guiqing even finished his sentence, everyone in the audience burst out laughing. Yingzhi also laughed. She really liked the way this guy named Guiqing spoke.

Guiqing leaped up onto the stage in one fell swoop. He rubbed his head as he asked, "What should we sing? I'm not sure what songs I know."

Everyone in the audience laughed again. Baldy said, "Then just sing 'Understand My Heart.' You sang that before when we were playing cards!"

As they made a scene over the song, the audience began to swell as more people gathered around to catch the action. Even those guests who were inside the house came out to see. Sanhuo couldn't have been more pleased by the audience's reaction. He leaned over to whisper to Yingzhi, "Yingzhi, it's all up to you now. Try to turn up the sexy a bit; that'll get them to request more songs."

Yingzhi understood what Sanhuo meant. She approached Guiqing and reached out to hold his hand, leading him to the center of the stage. She then had Wentang start the song. The audience laughed even louder; some of them even started to whistle.

Yingzhi put all her emotion into her duet with Guiqing. But when it was Guiqing's turn to sing a verse, she discovered that he was completely out of tune; he was so bad that he couldn't even get through the song. The laughter coming from the audience turned into a crazed frenzy and the whistles grew even louder. Guiqing grew nervous and couldn't even remember the words. Yingzhi whispered, "Don't be nervous, just follow my lead." Yingzhi helped him through the song, and as he sang his parts, she would alternately gaze deep into his eyes or gently rest her head on his shoulder. The way they seductively exchanged gazes made everyone in the audience break out into wave after wave of applause. When Yingzhi was in school, she would help her mother out in the fields whenever she went home for vacation. That's where she learned how to flirt with men. Now that she was on stage, she was able to easily put all that to use. The way she twisted her body and teased the audience raised the spirits of everyone there. Some people even started yelling, "Kiss!" "Guiqing, cop a feel!"

Sanhuo's face turned red with glee. He kept saying, "Yingzhi is really one amazing little siren, isn't she!"

Even more people started requesting songs. The music kept going all the time until the car carrying the bride arrived, but even then some people seemed more interested in requesting songs than seeing the bride. Everyone talked about how the village chief son's wedding was so much more grand and exciting than any other. The village chief received so many compliments that they started to go to his head; when it came time to settle up at the end of the night, he paid Sanhuo 800 yuan. That money also went right to Sanhuo's head, for he immediately took out a 100 yuan note and gave it to Yingzhi. When you combined that with the 48 yuan she made from song requests and the 5 yuan tip the village chief gave her earlier, Yingzhi came home that day with 153 yuan. She was utterly shocked. Never in her life had she held so much money in her hands, and she certainly never imagined it would be so easy to make that much money.

Yingzhi could sense that her life was about to change.

III

Yingzhi decided to go to the county seat to buy one or two skirts that she could wear for her performances. She had seen on television that most of the female pop stars wore revealing outfits. Yingzhi also wanted to purchase an outfit that would expose her shoulders, and a two-piece one that would show off her midriff. She knew that would win over even more members of the audience. When she shared her idea with Sanhuo, he clapped his hands together in support. "I was just about to talk to you about that! I've got an extra 50 yuan set aside for you if you can buy a semi-see-through skirt. Under your skirt you should wear one of those mini thongs; from now on you can't wear those grandma undies that most people in the countryside wear. What people in the country describe as 'smutty,' people in the city call 'sexy.' You should also buy some rouge to put on your face and some nice red lipstick; that'll really turn them on. You also need to learn to sing in a way that really tickles them in the right place, if you know what I mean. If you can do all that, you'll succeed! Yingzhi, I knew that I had a good eye when I picked you. I see great potential in you to make a ton of money!"

Yingzhi was ecstatic as she took the 50 yuan from Sanhuo. As he handed her the money, he smiled. "Yingzhi, I never knew you had such a nasty side."

Yingzhi took the money and headed toward the edge of the village. As she was walking away, she thought, *What business is it of yours whether I'm nasty? Don't you ever try taking advantage of me!*

It didn't take long at all for Yingzhi to find exactly what she was looking for at one of the boutique stores in the county seat. She spent nearly two hours haggling with the shopkeepers over prices, but in the end she got the price she wanted. She ended up spending less than 100 yuan for everything. Yingzhi thought it was the bargain of the century. She was so happy that she even bought herself two pink bras embroidered with flowery gold patterns. She tried one on at the store and liked it so much that she didn't even take it off. She walked out of that store standing tall with her chest out. Yingzhi felt more confident about herself than at any time ever before.

Yingzhi also opened a fixed-term savings account at the bank in the county seat. She started off with an initial deposit of 100 yuan. The little red deposit book she held in her hand seemed to send a burst of warmth straight to her heart. She wasn't sure where to keep it; finally she decided to just stuff it down her bra. Her new bra clamped her breasts so tightly that she though it was much safer to keep it there than in her pocket. Once she had the deposit book securely in place, she proudly strutted down the streets of the county seat. She could feel a fire burning in her chest. It had been only a few days since she graduated from high school, and Yingzhi was already the first person in her family to have their own savings account! Moreover, she didn't have to do any hard work to earn it! Yingzhi wondered what this meant; it meant, she finally decided, that she was resourceful. Being resourceful is something that comes naturally; it isn't something you can learn. Thinking about that gave her a great sense of pride; she felt that everyone on the street was looking at her with admiration, which made her stick her chest out even more.

Yingzhi was planning on getting on the bus to go home for lunch, but when she got to the bus station at the county seat, someone called her name. She turned to look and discovered it was the tall guy from Old Temple Village with whom she had sung the duet—Guiqing.

Guiqing was pushing a brand-new bicycle. He looked at Yingzhi with an expression of surprise and joy. That gave Yingzhi a feeling of great satisfaction.

"You came here for shopping?" Guiqing asked.

"That's right," said Yingzhi. "Did you just buy this bicycle?"

"Well," Guiqing explained, "after we sang that duet that day, I had a lucky streak and I've been winning money every day since then. After winning so much money, I was thinking about heading down to Phoenix Dike to take you out. I wanted to thank you for helping me turn my luck around that day! But your village is so far away. I figured that sooner or later I was going to have to buy a bicycle anyway, so I decided to just take my winnings and buy a bike now."

Yingzhi laughed. "You're pulling my leg! You're only saying that because you happened to run into me!"

Guiqing earnestly responded, "Only a bastard would lie like that. I was truly planning on going down to Phoenix Dike!"

Yingzhi giggled; the sound of her laughter was especially crisp. She replied, "Well . . . I guess you must be a bastard then!"

Yingzhi's laughter made Guiqing's ears burn; he couldn't refrain from reaching up to rub them. He smiled and asked, "Have you had lunch yet?"

"Not yet," Yingzhi responded. "Why? Are you treating?"

"If you are willing to join me, I'd be over the moon," said Guiqing.

Yingzhi didn't have anything pressing waiting for her to do at home, so she figured why not join him for lunch. After thinking it over for a moment, she replied, "Okay then, I never object to a free meal!"

Guiqing was ecstatic. "Okay then, I'll make sure this is just the first of many!"

There happened to be a small restaurant called Come Back Again right next to the bus station, and the two of them went in. It wasn't very crowded inside, and they found a table for two in the corner. Guiqing commented, "This is the best spot. It's as if they were just waiting for us to show up."

"Keep dreaming," Yingzhi sarcastically responded.

Guiqing asked Yingzhi to order, telling her to pick anything on the menu that she wanted. Yingzhi knew that he had just won some money, but she figured he couldn't possibly have won that much. She decided to order just two inexpensive dishes: stir-fried tofu and stir-fried shredded pork. Guiqing took one look and laughed. "That's it? If that's all you're going to order, you'd be better off going home to eat!" He took the menu from her and added a plate of salt-and-pepper shrimp and braised hare. Guiqing told Yingzhi that this restaurant was famous for its braised hare. He had it once here with Youjie, the village chief's son—he was the one who just got married.

Yingzhi had never eaten out in a restaurant before. Back when she was in school, she would use the rice provided by the student cafeteria to supplement the meals she packed from home. After school got out, she never thought to go to a restaurant to eat. It was only that day that she finally realized that restaurant food is actually a thousand times tastier than what she usually ate at home. Yingzhi focused entirely on the meal, while

Guiqing was consumed with talking nonstop. Guiqing said that he hadn't been back to school since middle school. He was the only son in his family; he also had a little sister in middle school at a boarding school. His family was fairly well off in the village because his father was a very capable man and even owned his own fruit orchard. They were considered one of the wealthier local families. He occasionally took part-time jobs doing remodels and construction, but when he felt too lazy for that, he would just hang out at home and help his dad. His family orchard was famous for its pears. They were the kind that didn't look very pretty on the outside but were especially sweet and tasty. They made good money every summer from their pear crop. His father had put all that money in the bank; he was saving up for Guiqing's wedding.

At that point in the story Guiqing suddenly stopped and flashed Yingzhi a strange look. Yingzhi thought the whole thing rather funny, and she wondered, *Don't tell me you invited me to lunch because you want me to marry you?* But Yingzhi just ignored the look he gave her and focused on gobbling down the braised hare. She intentionally kept repeating, "This is amazing! I never knew that rabbit could taste this good!" But after she said that, she started to feel sorry for the poor rabbit she was eating; she even wondered what color it had been.

After lunch Guiqing told Yingzhi that she didn't need to take the bus home; since the distance was only around a dozen *li*, he would take her on his bike. Yingzhi decided that wasn't a bad idea, and when she realized that she could save the bus fare, she immediately agreed. Yingzhi sat on the rear frame of Guiqing's bicycle.

The scenery out on the plains in autumn was gorgeous. Riding on a bicycle with the wind in your face and enjoying the view was a completely different experience than sitting on a crowded bus. Whenever they saw something interesting, they could immediately hop off the bike and check it out. Yingzhi's village wasn't that far away, but they spent a full two or three hours on the road.

As they approached Phoenix Dike, Yingzhi told Guiqing to get off the main road and take a small dirt path, which would be faster. She didn't realize that because a few days earlier there had been a downpour, which was followed by a few sunny days, that dirt path would be all jagged and uneven. Their bicycle kept violently bumping up and down. Sitting on the back of the bike, Yingzhi almost fell off several times. Finally she said, "I can't take this anymore. I'm getting off."

Guiqing quickly stopped. "I can't take it either. Nor can my bike!"

So they both got off the bike and started to walk. Yingzhi sighed and said, "Originally I thought this shortcut would save us some time, but now it looks like it will end up taking us even longer!"

Guiqing responded, "It's okay. It's nice to walk anyway. You have no idea how worried I was as we were riding."

"Worried about what?" Yingzhi asked.

Guiqing flashed her a naughty look and smiled, "You really want to know?"

"Just tell me," insisted Yingzhi.

"I was afraid that my little brother might be crushed after spending all that time on the bike," said Guiqing.

Yingzhi was completely confused. "What does your little brother have to do with it? And didn't you just say you only had a little sister?"

Guiqing broke out in laughter. "Yingzhi, you really don't understand what I was saying? Or are you just playing dumb?"

Yingzhi still had no idea what he was trying to say. When Guiqing saw how confused she looked, he laughed even harder. He finally pulled himself together enough to explain, "I'm the big brother, and *he* is my little brother!" He pointed to his crotch.

Yingzhi immediately turned red. It was as if all the blood in her body immediately rushed to her face. She said, "Now you're just being plain evil! I'm not talking to you!" Yingzhi began to run away from him.

Pushing his bike, Guiqing ran after her. "Yingzhi, I was just joking! No need to be like that!" Guiqing pleaded.

After running for a while, Yingzhi was completely out of energy and had to stop. By that time the dirt road had already converged with the river, and Phoenix Dike was right on the other side of the river. Yingzhi figured that since she was basically already home, she should just say goodbye and tell Guiqing to go back.

It had been difficult for Guiqing to chase after her while pushing his bike. When they finally stopped, he was panting for breath. His chest was heaving, and he was taking deep long breaths; even Yingzhi could feel his breath on her face. For some reason Yingzhi felt as if her entire body were burning up. It was as if those heavy breaths that Guiqing was exhaling were balls of fire that had ignited her. She suddenly changed her mind and decided she didn't want to go home right away.

"The scenery here in your village is really beautiful," said Guiqing. "But my village isn't too bad either!"

"Why should I care about the scenery in your village? So long as it's nice here, I'm happy," said Yingzhi.

"Well, the fact that we also have beautiful scenery in my village means that you'll be more willing to come visit me there," said Guiqing.

"Your village is nothing but a basket full of evil things. I have no interest in ever setting foot in that place," insisted Yingzhi.

Guiqing laughed. "And I suppose I'm the most evil thing in that basket?"

"And what if you are?" Yingzhi giggled.

As Yingzhi spoke, she gazed at Guiqing with a seductive and flirtatious look. Guiqing felt something well up inside him. He laid his bicycle on the ground and said, "Okay then, I'll admit it." As he spoke, he walked over to her, reached out his arms, and pulled her in close to him. Yingzhi immediately felt her body grow weak. She wanted to push his hands away, but nothing she did could free her from his embrace. She wanted to hit him, but she didn't have the strength even to raise her arms. She wanted to curse him, but by the time her curses made their way to her lips, they were almost inaudible. By then Guiqing's hands had already worked their way up to her breasts. Her entire body was taken over by a strange feeling of pleasure. She knew Guiqing was the reason she was feeling this way, and so she decided to stop struggling and give in. All she wanted was for that feeling of pleasure to last just a little bit longer. That is when Guiqing began kissing her on the lips. By then Yingzhi's initial resistance had transformed so that she was now taking the initiative. Just a moment before, when she tried to resist him, she had felt completely devoid of energy, but now all that energy had returned. Yingzhi used her tongue to nudge Guiqing's tongue back into his mouth, but then her tongue started exploring his mouth. As Guiqing let her do that, his hand went even deeper. Yingzhi began to moan. Guiqing led her over to a patch of grass beside the river and laid her down.

By that time the sun was getting ready to set. Although it was already autumn, the weather didn't really feel like autumn yet. Under the fading rays of the sun, the grass beside the river appeared green and lush. The glow of the setting sun stroked the lovers' bodies, gently caressing them before vanishing behind the clouds; as the sun disappeared, the colors of dusk quickly set in. By the time Guiqing's and Yingzhi's bodies separated from each other, the sky was already getting quite dark. The couple just lay there in the grass looking up at the dark sky.

It was only after a long time that Yingzhi finally broke the silence. "Is this what you would consider rape?"

"Hey, you were much more forceful than me," Guiqing protested. "If anyone was raped, it was me!"

Yingzhi thought about what just happened and couldn't help laughing. She had long heard about what happens between men and women but never imagined the real thing would be so much fun. She finally said, "Anyway, you're the one that seduced me!"

Seeing her laugh also made Guiqing laugh. "I guess I kind of seduced you. But that's only because I really like you. That day after we sang that duet, I even thought how great it would be if I could one day marry you."

"Keep dreaming," Yingzhi replied. "But you better be prepared, I require quite a few betrothal gifts. I'll need a house, a television set, a refrigerator, and, um, a washing machine . . . That's right, I'll also want a karaoke machine because you know how much I love to sing. So what do you say? Can you handle all that?"

"I guess I'll have to sell myself off, one chunk of flesh at a time. I'll take my meat down to the county seat to sell it. I think that's the only way I'll be able to afford you!" Guiqing joked.

Yingzhi burst out laughing at that and said, "So how much meat do you have on your bones to sell? Do really think it will bring a better price than the pig we have at home in our pen?" Her shoulders trembled as she laughed, and her breasts bounced up and down.

Guiqing laughed too. He was thinking about how beautiful Yingzhi was. He'd be willing to endure any torture imaginable if he were really able to marry her one day.

The evening wind carried the sound of their laughter along the river and to the other shore. The chimney smoke from town had already dispersed into the night air, and you could see lights coming from the windows of the houses just outside the village. Yingzhi was in great spirits. *Wow,* she thought, *so this is what it is like to be in the full bloom of youth.* And in that moment she felt happy and content.

IV

Yingzhi never actually planned on marrying Guiqing; she felt she was way too young to start thinking about marriage. Yingzhi was quite happy with her new job singing for the Sanhuo Band, and even more so because she was making some money. Although the Sanhuo Band didn't perform every day, whenever someone booked them for a gig, she was always able to bring in some cash. Yingzhi did some calculations and figured out that even if she sang only four times a month, based on the pay she got last time, she would be able to take home 600 yuan a month. Even if the pay were a bit lower, she was quite confident she could at least break 400. Yingzhi could give her family 50 yuan a month and save everything else. In one year she would be able to save up several thousand yuan. As far as Yingzhi was concerned, that was already an astronomical number. Just imagining that by this time next year she would be in control of several thousand yuan made Yingzhi so excited that she would wake up in the middle of the night with a great big smile on her face.

Yingzhi was still in this state of happiness when winter arrived. Whenever she went out to perform with Sanhuo's troupe, there was a lot of hard work involved, driving there, setting up the stage, and singing outside all day in the cold weather, but Yingzhi nevertheless thought things couldn't be better. Her status within her family also saw a big change thanks to all the extra money she brought home. Yingzhi's mother was often grinning from ear to ear, saying, "My daughter Yingzhi is brilliant. Thank goodness she didn't go to college; otherwise she would have ended up in debt just like Chunhui!" Yingzhi would always smile whenever she heard her mother say that. As far as she was concerned, everything her mother said was absolutely correct.

One day the wind was blowing violently and Yingzhi had to go to the bathroom. The bathroom was constructed out of a few pieces of plywood set up outside in the corner of the pigpen. The wind went right through the cracks between the plywood and whipped against her buttocks. It reminded her of how sometimes when she had her period it was so cold in there that she would be reluctant to change her pads. As she sat there squatting on two wooden planks, she suddenly realized that her period still hadn't come that month. Yingzhi started to get nervous. Two years earlier when her second aunt got pregnant, Yingzhi had asked her how she knew she was expecting. Her second aunt explained that you know you have a baby on the way when your period doesn't come. Squatting there with the cold wind whipping against her, Yingzhi thought about what her second aunt told her, and she could feel the goosebumps forming all over her body.

Yingzhi didn't dare go to the village health clinic and instead took a trip to the county hospital for an exam. She was extremely depressed to learn that she was indeed pregnant. She was also a bit confused. She had had sex with Guiqing only a few times. He frequently came to see her, but most of the time other people were around, so it was hard for them to find opportunities to be alone. There was that one time, though, when Yingzhi went out to Fangjiatai for a performance and Guiqing went with her. At one point when she went to the bathroom, Guiqing followed behind her. He was so anxious to be with her that he insisted on leading her out to a patch of forest behind someone's house and they did it there. The whole thing was quite rushed and took only a few minutes. There was something about that time that made Yingzhi quite unhappy; she even sharply admonished Guiqing, saying, "How could you behave like such a hooligan!"

Yingzhi knew that must have been the day she got pregnant. Just thinking about it made her furious. She wished that she could chop Guiqing up with a knife. Yingzhi went directly from the county hospital to Old Temple Village to look for Guiqing. He was in the middle of a mah-jongg game, but he was thrilled to see Yingzhi. He immediately tossed his mah-jongg tiles aside and followed her outside. She looked upset and just kept walking; Guiqing followed behind her. They walked all the way to the forest at the edge of the village, and only then did Yingzhi finally stop.

"I thought you decided you weren't interested in me anymore," said Guiqing.

Yingzhi didn't look happy. "You actually think I'm interested in you?"

Guiqing giggled. "If you aren't interested in me, then why did you come out to my village? I'm sure that you miss me, but you're just too embarrassed to admit it. Isn't that right? Actually, this forest is a good spot for us to do it."

"Fuck you!" blurted out Yingzhi.

Guiqing was taken aback. "What's wrong? Don't tell me that you came all the way out here just to yell at me?"

"Yelling at you isn't going to change how pissed off I am!" said Yingzhi.

"What happened?" asked Guiqing. "Did your mom discover that we slept together?"

Yingzhi still wanted to yell at him, but she decided to take a different approach. What was the purpose of yelling at him anyway? She instead softened her tone. "It's much worse than that."

"Did you hook up with a new boyfriend? And he found out about me?" Guiqing guessed.

"Screw you!" Yingzhi retorted before finally telling him the truth: "I didn't get my period this month."

"And what does that disgusting stuff have to do with me?" asked Guiqing.

Yingzhi lost her temper. "The reason I didn't get my period is because I'm pregnant with your bastard child! And you have the nerve to ask what it has to do with you!"

"What?" Guiqing was visibly shocked. "You're pregnant? And it's my child?"

"You are such an asshole! If it's not yours, who the hell do you think it belongs to?" yelled Yingzhi.

Guiqing immediately stamped his feet and clapped his hands. His face lit up with a huge smile. "That's great news! Amazing! I never thought that I'd nail it like that!"

"You're actually happy? What about me? If people find out, how am I supposed to be able to face anyone?" Yingzhi moaned.

"You're going to be the mother of my son," replied Guiqing. "There is nothing shameful about that. Marry me and everything will be fine."

Yingzhi flashed him a cold smile. "And how exactly do you plan on marrying me?"

Guiqing remembered what Yingzhi had told him about her expectations for a betrothal gift, which immediately took the wind out of his sails. But then he seemed to realize something; he smirked and said, "I plan to leverage my son to marry you.

Don't tell me a television set and a washing machine are worth more than him?"

Yingzhi had been pondering what else she should press Guiqing for, but then she heard the word "son" and everything changed. A strange feeling welled up in her heart—she wasn't sure if it was hatred or joy. But she responded coldly to Guiqing. "You really know how to get your way!"

When Guiqing saw that response, he smiled. There was something naughty, almost sinister, about that smile. Guiqing said, "There is no other way. I think the earlier we get married the better."

"You're delusional!" Yingzhi yelled in anger.

Guiqing still had a smile on his face as he shot back, "Okay then, let's see what you do. Things will be just fine for me; but you are a woman, and things are different for women than for men. You know very well what kind of shame unmarried pregnant women face."

Yingzhi clenched her jaw with such anger that she almost broke a tooth. She wanted to curse him to hell, but then she thought about what Guiqing had said: she was indeed a woman. That's right, Yingzhi realized, I'm nothing but a woman. All the sins of romance and infidelity in the world are caused by men, but women are always the ones to get the blame. It seems as though that's the way things have been throughout history. If Guiqing were to decide to pretend none of this ever happened and try to completely avoid responsibility, what would she do? Just thinking about what would happen once news of her pregnancy spread around the village and imagining what it would be like if everyone started pointing and staring at her made Yingzhi tremble. She looked at Guiqing's arrogant face and decided to let go of the anger that had filled her heart. Instead, running through her heart was now nothing but a faint sadness, and it was all because she was a woman.

Guiqing took advantage of Yingzhi's sadness to pull her into his arms. He spoke to her in a particularly soft and caring voice. "Think of it as me begging you, Will you marry me?" And then he started getting touchy-feely with her again. Yingzhi was moved by his soft side, and she realized that she already belonged to him, so what else could she do?

V

It was the eighteenth day of the twelfth month of the lunar calendar and the weather was dark and overcast; it looked as if it might snow. As soon as you opened the door, the cold surged in. The wind was also particularly vicious; it raged like a pack of wild wolves, making everyone cringe. That was the day that Yingzhi was married off to Old Temple Village. She was already three months pregnant by then and knew that if she were going to get married, it was now or never; but Yingzhi viewed her marriage with a sense of resignation. Her pregnancy also took away her bargaining power when it came to her betrothal gifts.

Guiqing's family hired the Sanhuo Band to perform at the wedding. Sanhuo lamented the fact that after Yingzhi had let herself get knocked up, her absence meant that his revenue had been virtually cut in half. The Sanhuo Band set up in Old Temple Village and performed for the entire day. It was only at dusk that Yingzhi finally arrived in a tractor that Guiqing had hired for the occasion. As the tractor came blaring into Old Temple Village, Yingzhi heard that familiar music as soon as she reached the village entrance, and in that moment the tears began to well up in her eyes.

That night Guiqing had too much to drink. He was completely drunk by the time he entered the bridal chamber. He couldn't tell north from south, let alone manage to show any intimacy toward his new wife. Yingzhi lay there on her new bed, which was now soiled by the stench of alcohol, and wondered how she had ended up there. She kept going through the past in her mind, and by the middle of the night her pillow was soaked with tears.

Even though they were able to gain a daughter-in-law without spending much money, Guiqing's parents didn't seem very pleased. They both were rather cold toward Yingzhi. She, of course, could sense their lukewarm attitude, which made her even more depressed; but even more than that, she couldn't understand why they would be like that. Yingzhi asked Guiqing, "I didn't make your parents break the bank for the wedding, so why do they look so miserable?" Guiqing stammered over his words as he tried to answer her. Finally, he just gave up and told her the truth: "My parents said that any daughter-in-law who comes so cheap must not be any good. My mom even asked if you might have some kind of disease to allow yourself to be sold off for so little. I tried to explain to them what happened, but they wouldn't believe me."

What Guiqing said made Yingzhi so angry that she wanted to spit blood in his face. She wished she could just poison herself and end it all. She pounded the bed with her fist and started making accusations against Guiqing's parents. "So I'm cheap! I've made more money than your parents have even seen! Marrying into your family is the shittiest thing that has ever happened to me in my life! I guess after I met you, I had no choice but to sell myself off for a cheap price. But whether your family is good or bad, you have to have some sense of gratitude. How could they say such terrible things?"

Guiqing responded, "What are you yelling about? I've already explained your side of the story to them. That's just how old folks are. When they see that their daughter-in-law is different from those of other families, there is bound to be some gossip. My uncle's family is much better off than our family, but when his second son got married, the bride's family agreed only on the condition that my uncle's daughter married into their family. My parents had been really worried about my marriage prospects, and for a long time they ate only two meals a day so that they could save every penny for my wedding. They even said that if they couldn't get enough money together, they would use my sister to do a marriage exchange like my uncle's family. So it was a good thing that I met you; we were able to bring you into the family without spending too much money. But everything played out so fast that my parents haven't had a chance to readjust their thinking. They couldn't figure out why you would be willing to marry into our family for so little money. It's all quite simple, isn't it?"

Yingzhi was so furious that she felt as if she were going to explode. At the same time, she was at a loss to explain how she was feeling, so instead they just ended up screaming at each other. Sick of trying to explain himself, Guiqing resorted to silence or simple one-sentence responses; he acted as if the whole thing were just a big headache that he didn't need. Yingzhi yelled so much that her throat grew hoarse. She was exhausted by the whole affair, and her stomach was bothering her. Afraid that she might hurt the baby, she decided not to argue anymore. Not long after they stopped arguing, she started to feel that her entire marriage was just one big joke. Guiqing was a thousand times more boring than she could ever have imagined, and now, in the blink of an eye, her in-laws had become her psychological enemies.

Yingzhi knew how to perform on stage, but she didn't know how to do that in her everyday life. The hatred she had for her in-laws was written all over her face every time she saw them. When she spoke to them, their interactions always had a passive-aggressive tinge. And even the slightest happening in the village, whether it be a rooster flying or a dog jumping, would be ample excuse for her to go outside to check out what was going on. When she returned, she would just walk around the house singing sappy love songs, acting as if her in-laws, with whom she lived under the same roof, didn't even exist.

But Yingzhi's in-laws were no pushovers. As the elders of the house, they felt that their new daughter-in-law should be deferential and wait on them hand and foot. She should cook, clean, tend to the livestock, and take care of all the various chores both inside and outside the house. As far as they were concerned, she should be constantly exchanging pleasantries with them, pouring them tea, and heating up hot water for them to soak their feet in—*that* is how a true daughter-in-law would behave. Otherwise, what was the point of bringing her into the family? Just to pop out some babies? As long as their son had even a scrap of talent, he could find someone to produce a bunch of babies! Her family didn't just consist of a husband: there was also her mother-in-law, father-in-law, and sister-in-law, so how could she possibly act with such arrogance? After thinking about it, her in-laws also began to openly display their displeasure. Sometimes they would be chatting and giggling with their daughter, and as soon as Yingzhi entered the room, they would immediately quiet down and draw long faces. One night Yingzhi told Guiqing, "Every morning before I go out, I always see two horses."

Guiqing asked, "What do you mean? We don't have any horses . . ."

"Then I guess you haven't taken a good look at your parents' faces," said Yingzhi. "Their faces are even longer than a horse's."

Guiqing responded only with a simple "Fuck!" It was hard to tell if he was commenting on Yingzhi's sharp tongue or his parents' long horselike faces.

Summer had just passed when Yingzhi's baby was born. It was a boy. He had large wide eyes and a loud healthy cry. Yingzhi's in-laws were so happy to welcome a baby boy to the family that they busied themselves around the house doing god knows what. When they went to the hospital, the in-laws' long horselike faces magically became much shorter as soon as they saw Yingzhi holding their new grandson in her arms. The two white-haired grandparents leaned in to see their grandson, caressing his little face with their coarse hands; they were so happy, they couldn't stop smiling. Meanwhile, Yingzhi maintained her indifferent attitude toward them, thinking, *Now that I bore you a grandson, let's see if you dare to keep treating me with such an attitude.*

When the baby turned one month old, Guiqing hosted a banquet to celebrate his son's arrival. Guiqing was quite proud to be a father. But when it came to Yingzhi, that pride turned into arrogance. After he had stuffed himself at the banquet and drank his full, Guiqing lay in bed using his fingers to pick out the food residue stuck between his teeth as he shamelessly told Yingzhi, "Do you really think you could ever have borne me an amazing son like this if I hadn't perfectly nailed it when we fucked?"

Yingzhi cursed him. "You are absolutely shameless!"

Guiqing didn't say anything, but he thought, *It takes two people to be shameless! It's a good thing I'm so shameless, because that's the only way I was able to lock you down; it took putting a son in your belly to get you to commit to me. If I was so concerned about things like respectability, I might not even be married yet!* The more he thought about it, the more arrogant he became. Guiqing thought what he had managed to pull off was actually quite amazing.

It finally came time for Yingzhi to return to her parents' house to visit. It would be the first time she returned home since giving birth. She didn't want to look like a loser in front of her parents, so she made herself up before going home. Although Yingzhi was already a mother, she was still a young girl not yet twenty years old; her face had a youthful rosy hue, and if it hadn't been for her engorged breasts, she would still look like a teenage girl. Yingzhi stood in front of the mirror admiring her looks, but eventually she couldn't help heaving a deep sigh. She thought she should have had a long and happy period of youth traveling all over with the Sanhuo Band singing songs. She may even have been able to mold herself into a beloved pop star that everyone fawned on; if not that, she could at least have dated a bit more before settling down. She used to have a bunch of male admirers that she hung around and flirted with—even that would have made her incomparably happier than her current situation. But . . . but . . . but she somehow foolishly allowed herself to get pregnant with Guiqing's child, and just like that, it was as if her youth had been suddenly ripped away from her. Yingzhi caressed her face and felt a surging wellspring of emotions.

Yingzhi was lost in thought when she suddenly heard her son crying. Her son's name was Jianhuo, which meant "trash" or "cheap goods." The child's grandfather had picked out the name. At first Yingzhi protested, "Why should my son be stuck with a name like Jianhuo? I don't want my child to be referred to as 'trash'!" Her father-in-law explained, "That is the old custom. If you give a lowly name to a child, he'll have an easier upbringing. If you give him a precious or fancy name, it will only bring him harm. Do you understand?" Her mother-in-law chimed in, "When Guiqing was a baby, we called him 'Sweet Potato.' It was only after he turned eighteen that we started calling him Gui-qing, and look at how strong and healthy he turned out!" Ying-zhi was so angry, she clenched her teeth; she initially didn't want to go along with her in-laws' suggestion, but thinking that a good name might bring him misfortune, she decided to agree to it after all. As soon as she made that compromise, she felt as if she had been forced to wear a pair of shoes that were too small and had a sharp pebble inside—the discomfort was unbearable.

Whenever Jianhuo cried, Yingzhi knew that he needed to be changed. Jianhuo would pee all the time, so much so that the entire house smelled of piss. As Yingzhi got up to change his diaper, she cursed under her breath, "That's right; piss, piss, piss. Piss yourself to death! All you do is piss! You really are a little piece of trash!" She would get extremely frustrated every time she had to change his diaper and had the urge to give him a good slap on the butt. She raised her arm to hit him, but instead she give him a gentle caress. Jianhuo's body was soft and fleshy like a sponge; it felt good to touch his skin, and after caressing him for a moment, Yingzhi no longer had the urge to hit him.

"Shit, it really stinks in here," Guiqing complained as he stepped into the room. "Yingzhi, there is something I want to discuss with you."

Yingzhi responded with annoyance. "I'm sure it isn't anything good. Anyway, let's hear it!"

"Not necessarily," said Guiqing. "Here's the deal: my parents have been hoping for a grandson for a long time now. Now that you have given them Jianhuo, they are so ecstatic, they don't know what to do with themselves. They suggested that they help raise Jianhuo with us. What do you think?"

Yingzhi thought, *They look down on me and now all of sudden they've come groveling for a favor? There's no way I'm letting them get what they want!* "Forget it! I gave birth to him. On what basis should I hand my child over to them? If your mother wants a grandson, tell her to give birth to her own!"

Guiqing laughed. "If my mom gave birth again, it would be a son, not a grandson! As far as this family goes, you're the only one who can give them a grandson!"

Yingzhi didn't laugh; she was still dead set on going against her mother-in-law. Yingzhi said, "I don't give a shit about this son or grandson business. All I know is that he's *my* son and I'll be the one raising him! They have no right to lay a finger on him!"

"Where is this stubbornness coming from?" Guiqing pleaded. "Just think about how much easier it will be for us if my parents help us watch the baby. At the very least, we wouldn't have to put up with this piss smell in our room all the time! All this fucking kid does is piss and shit!"

"Well, even if he pisses and shits all the time, he's still my son and I like it! You got a problem with that?"

After getting repeatedly pecked on by Yingzhi, Guiqing became upset and said, "Okay, okay! We'll do it your way! But after you get tired of looking after him, don't complain to me about how difficult it is. I'm going out tonight to play mah-jongg. I tried to make things easier for you, but you don't seem to want the help. So be it! You really fucking live up to the name of being the mother of 'trash'!"

Since Yingzhi was getting ready to visit her parents, she wasn't in the mood to continue arguing with Guiqing. She knew it wouldn't look good if she and her husband weren't on speaking terms when she visited home. So she decided to respond to Guiqing's insults with a simple "Humph," pick up the baby, and go out the door. Once she was outside, Yingzhi turned around to see if Guiqing was coming with her, but instead she saw her in-laws standing in the doorway staring at her; they both looked a bit sad. She knew that they were gazing at Jianhuo, which made her feel quite smug. She held Jianhuo tighter and leaned over to plant two little kisses on his face: "Muh, muh." She then turned and strutted away from the village.

By the time the couple arrived at Yingzhi's parents' house, it was already midday. Yingzhi's parents, brothers, and two sisters-in-law all came out to see Jianhuo; they agreed that the baby indeed had a trashy name but that his facial features had all the auspicious signs. Guiqing and Yingzhi both laughed. Sanhuo also came by and handed them a 100 yuan note. He said it was for Jianhuo and they should consider it a first greeting present. When Yingzhi's parents saw the present, they insisted that Sanhuo stay for dinner.

They set up two tables in their main room. Guiqing and Yingzhi's brothers started drinking as soon as they sat down, and it didn't take long for them to start getting rowdy. Guiqing was a person who couldn't stop drinking once he got a whiff of alcohol. He would continue until he was flat-out drunk. And once he was drunk, Guiqing had a tendency to say all kinds of crazy and irresponsible things, but he always had a knack for making the people around him laugh. Sitting at the other table, Yingzhi didn't even try to mask how annoyed she was with Guiqing, but there was nothing she could do.

Since he was a generation older and he didn't drink, Sanhuo sat with Yingzhi and her parents. As they talked, Yingzhi kept asking how the Sanhuo Band was doing; she wanted to know about when and where all the recent performances were held and how much money they made. As she listened to Sanhuo talk about the troupe, she kept sighing. Sanhuo bragged about all the things the band had been up to; he also heaved a deep sigh of regret about what a shame it was that Yingzhi had to leave the troupe after such a short time. Yingzhi's parents had no interest in what songs the Sanhuo Band had been singing.

Instead, they just kept asking their daughter how things had been with Guiqing's parents. Yingzhi had a lot to say about her in-laws. After viciously attacking them for a while, she naturally got around to talking about how they wanted to raise Jianhuo. Yingzhi said, "I refuse to let them lay a finger on their grandson! That'll piss them off!"

Sanhuo said, "Yingzhi, let me say a word. You're always doing all kinds of stupid things. The way you blindly rushed to get married and have a child was stupid, and now the way you are so stubbornly dead set on preventing your in-laws from helping you take care of the baby is also stupid."

"How is that stupid?" Yingzhi protested. "Anyway, I don't want to do anything that might allow them to get their way!"

"It is good to take a firm stance on certain things, but you have to ask yourself if that approach is getting you anywhere. I don't see how your stance on this is to your benefit," Sanhuo explained. "If you prevent your in-laws from watching your child, you're the one who is going to end up taking care of him all the time. You're going to be exhausted, and you'll be stuck in the house; you won't be able to go out anywhere. You'll be like a lamb tied to a leash. Jianhuo will become a burden tying you down."

Yingzhi thought about it but she still protested, "They are so mean to me, why shouldn't I make them suffer a bit?"

"Why do you need to think of things from that perspective? Don't worry about them, worry about yourself! Let your in-laws take care of the baby, and you can do whatever the hell you want! You can go out and have fun! If you're interested, you can even rejoin the band to sing with us and make some extra pocket money! What's wrong with that?"

Now that Sanhuo had put that idea out there, Yingzhi thought it made sense. *That's right, why should I be so intent on making them miserable? I should instead be worrying about making myself happy! And if I can rejoin the Sanhuo Band, I might even be able to get my youth back!*

Yingzhi immediately asked Sanhuo, "Can I really rejoin the band?"

"Why not?" replied Sanhuo. "You've still got a good voice and a young, pretty face. If you can slim down a bit around the waist, you'll look just like you did before the baby!"

Yingzhi's face turned red with joy. "Really? Are you sure? I can really come back?"

Sanhuo cracked up laughing. "Well, it's not totally up to me. Talk it over with your parents."

Yingzhi's mother said, "Our girl Yingzhi has always been so full of energy. Even though she had a baby, she still doesn't act like a typical married woman. She's more like a single young woman!"

But Yingzhi's father had a different take on things. "I'm afraid it won't go over well. Once you are married, you have to listen to your husband's family. I'm sure your in-laws would be upset if you ran around putting yourself out there like that. I don't think it is a good idea."

"What's there to be afraid of?" Yingzhi asked. "They have looked down on me since the day I married into their family. Anyway, I hope it pisses them off!"

Guiqing was already so drunk that he was on the floor; he didn't even have the ability to carry on with his bullshit. Yingzhi asked her brothers to help carry Guiqing into the bedroom so that he could lie down. Guiqing looked a bit sad in his drunken state; he kept making a dissatisfied snorting sound. Yingzhi was so annoyed by him that she just cast him a sidelong glance but didn't have the patience to check on how he was doing. Instead, she pulled out an old wooden chest to look for those outfits she used to wear as a singer before she married.

It had been only a few short months since she stopped singing, and although her outfits still looked as bright and dazzling as ever, they already smelled of mildew. Even thought it was cold out, Yingzhi couldn't resist holding them up to her body to see if they still fit. She then took off her cotton jacket and removed her sweater and her long underwear. When she got down to her bra and panties, she began to shiver. Trembling from the cold, she slipped into one of her sexy stage outfits and looked at herself in the mirror. Her breasts were fuller after having a baby, and the dress really helped accentuate her cleavage. Yingzhi thought this outfit would be even more tantalizing once she was back on stage. The waist was a bit tight, but that wasn't a big deal. She still looked gorgeous in that dress. Yingzhi stood before the mirror striking all kinds of sexy poses and flashing a seductive smile.

It took but a few seconds for her to regain her confidence. She decided, *Okay then, I'll let them take care of Jianhuo and I'll find my own happiness.*

VI

Yingzhi came down with a cold the day she returned home. She suspected that she must have caught a chill while trying on those fancy outfits. Guiqing was unusually considerate in the way he brought her water to drink with her medicine and almost carried her to the bed so that she could lie down. To prevent Jianhuo from catching his mom's cold, Guiqing even brought the baby to his parents so that they could take care of him. Yingzhi observed all this with a cold eye, but now that she had a plan, she was resigned to everything else. She didn't say a word and just lay there completely devoid of energy.

Since Yingzhi was so young and in such good health, her cold was no big deal. It took her only three days to get right back to her old self. In fact, to Yingzhi's satisfaction, she seemed to have lost some weight while she was sick. Yingzhi was even happier when she discovered that her waist was a bit thinner.

When Guiqing saw that his wife didn't object to his taking Jianhuo to his parents, he seemed to really light up. He heaved a sigh of relief that Yingzhi was finally facing reality. He immediately got right back to his old way of life, which meant hanging out in the village with his buddies during the day and drinking and gambling at night—he left all the household duties to Yingzhi.

Yingzhi let her in-laws take care of Jianhuo, and except for breastfeeding she hardly spent any time with the baby. Jianhuo even slept in the same bed with his grandmother at night. But Yingzhi got to enjoy that life for just two days, because on the third day her father-in-law called her to help out in the orchard. He said, "You're mother-in-law is helping you watch the baby, so you should pitch in with the other work. You've got nothing else to do anyway."

Yingzhi was shocked. "How could you ask me to work in the orchard? What about Guiqing?"

Her father-in-law explained, "Guiqing has never done this kind of labor. He'd have no idea what to do."

Yingzhi flashed him a cold smile. "Well, neither do I! It's not like I've ever done that kind of labor either."

"You can learn," her father-in-law explained.

"So why doesn't Guiqing learn?" retorted Yingzhi.

"He's never been willing to learn," her father-in-law said.

"Well, neither am I," said Yingzhi.

The look on her father-in-law's face hardened. "What are you talking about? Guiqing is a man. Men his age should be out there eating, drinking, and having fun. Who would ever respect him if he spent all day out here in the orchard working? You are Guiqing's woman; you need to learn to love and respect him."

Yingzhi smirked as she replied, "Haven't you heard that we have gender equality these days? In the new society, men and women are equal. If men want to go out and have fun, then women should be able to do that too. And if women can work hard, so can men!"

Her father-in-law almost screamed, "What the hell are you talking about! Take a look around this village and tell me which households don't have their women out there working in the fields? Which households don't allow the men of the house to go out and have some fun? Once I'm dead, he will be the head of this household. If he doesn't have his fun now, when will he?"

"I've never heard of such a thing!" Yingzhi was at a loss.

Her father-in-law started to yell even louder. He was now screaming at the top of his lungs. "Our family has always followed this rule! If you're part of our family, you will follow it too!"

The whole time they were arguing, Yingzhi's mother-in-law had been standing in the doorway holding Jianhuo. It was at that moment she finally jumped in to the conversation. "Don't worry, you can stop going out to the fields when your son gets married and your daughter-in-law bears you a grandson! This is how it is for women. That's how have I lived my life. You're a woman too, so start acting like a woman!"

Yingzhi had never seen her father-in-law act like this and was actually somewhat intimidated. She didn't dare speak back to him. She silently cursed her in-laws, thinking, *Why should I have to live the same kind of life you have lived? Why can't I do things my way? What the hell do you even know about what kind of life a woman should live?*

Although Yingzhi must have protested a thousand times over, in the end she went with her father-in-law. It was freezing out, and the cold wind cut straight to her bones. The family orchard was outside the village; to get there they had to walk along the river for several *li*. The grass along the river was all dead and yellow, lazily strewn flat on the ground. The cold wind blew along the surface of the river, caressing the dead grass and sneaking down under her collar. Yingzhi didn't have a hat or a scarf on, and the cotton-lined jacket she was wearing was one of the thin ones because she thought the thicker ones looked frumpy; but that meant that every time the wind blew, she would huddle

in a little ball. That also caused her to secretly think even more
wicked thoughts about her in-laws. Just as she was cursing them,
they came upon the forest where she and Guiqing had made
love. All of a sudden those memories welled up, causing her to
now aim her psychological gun at Guiqing—the terrible things
she wished on him left her mentally exhausted.

It turned out that there was nothing for her to do at the damn
orchard. Her father-in-law just walked around the property, all
the while ignoring Yingzhi. Later he began trimming some of
the branches, but Yingzhi had nothing to do except stand there
in the cold. Finally, Yingzhi said, "If you don't have any chores for
me, I'll go wait in the shed." Her father-in-law didn't respond.
Yingzhi let out a grumble and headed toward the straw shed.

Usually vacant, the shed was used only when the trees started
to bear fruit, and it was then that they worried about thieves
camping out there. But it seemed that some stray dogs had been
in there or perhaps a couple had used the place for secret hook-
ups; inside, it was a complete mess and reeked something terrible. Yingzhi got to the entrance and was so disgusted by the
stench inside that she failed to go in and even took a few steps
back. She turned to look at her father-in-law, who was still
focused on clipping branches and wasn't even looking in her
direction. Yingzhi stood there for a moment unsure what to do
when she noticed a broom beside the door. She picked it up, and
holding the broom in one hand and pinching her nose with the
other, she went inside and started haphazardly sweeping up all
the garbage littering the floor.

Once Yingzhi had cleaned up the shed, she huddled on the
floor holding her knees to her chest to stay warm. Through the
opening between the door and the wall she could see her father-
in-law in the distance still wielding his pair of clippers. Yingzhi
thought, *So I guess they volunteered to watch Jianhuo so that they*

could punish me by turning me into their slave! Well, I'm not standing for it! Just thinking about it made Yingzhi clench her teeth so hard they almost cracked.

Yingzhi still hadn't returned from the orchard when Sanhuo came by her in-laws' house to call on her. The first thing he did when he arrived was to walk around the property to check the place out. Seeing it, he really thought that Yingzhi must have been crazy to marry into a family this poor. Given her good looks, she could have done much better. There were absolutely no signs that Guiqing's family had any money. The house was old and beaten up; it must have been built by someone from Guiqing's grandfather's generation. Their courtyard was also rather dilapidated, and piled up near the corner of the wall was a bunch of old tiles that looked as if they were to be used for a new roof.

Yingzhi's mother-in-law was sitting in the courtyard holding Jianhuo. She was humming an old drum song melody to the baby. Sanhuo recognized Jianhuo and approached the child's grandmother to ask if Yingzhi was home.

Yingzhi's mother-in-law wouldn't say whether Yingzhi was home but just stared at Sanhuo suspiciously and started to grill him with questions. Her questions started to piss off Sanhuo, and he raised his voice to ask, "Do you know who I am? Yingzhi refers to me as her uncle! When Yingzhi married your son, it was my Sanhuo Band that performed at their wedding! Since I know her, I charged you only half my normal price. Do you remember now? And here you're looking at me like I'm some bad guy trying to seduce your daughter-in-law!"

It was a good thing that Guiqing had just lost money gambling and happened to come home to grab some cash; when he saw Sanhuo standing there getting upset with his mom, he quickly cleared up the misunderstanding. But as soon as Sanhuo learned that Yingzhi was out working in the orchard while Guiqing was gambling, he turned blue with rage. He yelled at Guiqing, scolding, "You should feel lucky that Yingzhi married a man like you! How could a grown man like you go off and have fun while his wife is out doing manual labor in the fields?"

Guiqing put his hands together and bowed slightly out of politeness and said that he had no idea that his father had asked Yingzhi to help out at the orchard. It was such a cold day, and there wasn't anything so pressing that needed to be done that couldn't wait.

Sanhuo didn't have the patience to waste his breath on Guiqing, but he left him with a message to pass on to his wife: "Tell Yingzhi to meet us tomorrow at ten in the morning at Yellow Leaf Swamp, and tell her not to forget to bring her stage clothes." With that, he hopped on his bicycle and peddled away.

Guiqing had been on a losing streak for the past several days. He had already gambled away what little money his family had. He also lost several games that very day and was now in debt for several hundred yuan. Guiqing was about to ask his parents if he could borrow some cash, but after hearing what Sanhuo said, he got a different idea. Guiqing knew that once Yingzhi got back on stage, she'd make a killing; he'd be able to repay his debt and still have money left over. Once he realized that, Guiqing was practically jumping for joy. He immediately ran off shouting, "Do you have any idea how much money Yingzhi will be able to bring in?"

Yingzhi's mother-in-law coldly responded, "That guy who came by here who runs that music group is bad news. It took only one look for me to see that. Aren't you worried he might try to take advantage of Yingzhi if you let her go out with his troupe?"

"That's impossible! Yingzhi looks at him like an uncle. They're from the same village. You know the old saying 'The rabbit never eats the grass beside its nest,'" said Guiqing.

Yingzhi's mother-in-law responded, "Even if he doesn't go after her, I'm sure that flirty little bitch will offer herself to him!"

Guiqing laughed. "She is a flirty little bitch, but she needs a guy like me to flirt with. If she ends up running off with someone, I'm sure it would be some strapping young lad and not an old man like him."

"I know more about slutty women and promiscuous men than you," Yingzhi's mother-in-law replied. "A young lad like you might have muscle and brawn, but an old fox like that guy is cunning and has all kinds of tricks."

Guiqing laughed even harder. "Wow, Mom, I'm really impressed. I never knew you understood so much about this stuff!"

Guiqing was still laughing when Yingzhi returned. As soon as Yingzhi heard Guiqing laughing, she immediately thought about how she had just been outside working in the cold, and her face turned red with anger. When Guiqing saw Yingzhi enter the house, he didn't wait for her to lose her temper but instead rushed over to her and in a playful childlike voice said, "My dear Yingzhi, my very own personal god of wealth, I see you have finally returned! While you were gone, your Uncle Sanhuo came to see you!"

Yingzhi was just about to start barking at Guiqing, but as soon as she heard that Sanhuo had visited, her temper was quelled. Yingzhi anxiously asked, "Did Uncle Sanhuo say what he came for?"

"Of course," replied Guiqing. "He asked you to show up tomorrow morning at ten at Yellow Leaf Swamp. He must want you to sing with the Sanhuo Band again. You need to negotiate your fee with him."

Yingzhi couldn't have been happier. "Really? He wants me to sing tomorrow?"

"Why would I lie?" said Guiqing. "You should go to bed early tonight so that you have enough energy for tomorrow's performance. I'll be the first in line to support you!"

But Yingzhi knew exactly what he was thinking. She rolled her eyes before saying, "Do you really think I'm going hand over my hard-earned money so that you can gamble it away? I'm warning you, don't even think it!"

Guiqing didn't dare try arguing with her; he was afraid that if he completely burned his bridges with Yingzhi, he would never see a single cent of her money. Instead, he put on a naughty face and smiled. "I wouldn't dare! The thought never crossed my mind! I wouldn't think about it even in my wildest dreams; not even in my wet dreams either!" But deep down Guiqing was thinking, *Once you have money, how could you possibly refuse to help me repay my debts? I'm the head of this household; that means I'm the one who's in charge. You're just my woman—you belong to me, so naturally your money belongs to me too!* Thinking about it like that put Guiqing at ease.

Although she had worked all day at the orchard and spent all that time pissed off, Yingzhi was now in a pretty good mood. She also had no intention of making her relationship with Guiqing worse because she knew she needed his support if she wanted to go out to sing with the troupe. That night she used another, calmer method to deal with the tension that had been building between them. Once Guiqing was sound asleep, Yingzhi suddenly realized that was the most at peace she had felt since the day she married into Old Temple Village.

VII

Yingzhi woke up early the next morning and made herself up. Guiqing lay in bed staring at Yingzhi as she got ready and put on her makeup. He watched as she transformed from a frumpy village housewife to a gorgeous siren radiating with seductive beauty. Guiqing couldn't help but feel a bit sour; it was as if his own wife were getting ready to go off and marry someone else. Guiqing said, "Yingzhi, there is something I have to make clear. You can sing all you want, but don't you dare mess around with anyone. You're *my* wife now."

Yingzhi's expression immediately turned. "Fuck you! You spend every day out and about fooling around, and now you're accusing me of messing around! When have I ever fooled around?"

"I've already got you to mess around with, so why would I need anyone else? And as for you, now that you've managed to use your charms to entrap me, you've already got what you wanted. You're mother of my child."

"Anyway, I'll do whatever Uncle Sanhuo tells me to do, and you'll have no say in it!" declared Yingzhi.

"Sure, so when you're out, Sanhuo will call the shots; but here at home, I call the shots. Right now you're at home, so you need to listen to me! When you're a young girl and get flirty, that is considered charming—it's even beautiful. But when a married woman gets flirty, that is considered deceptive; it is intentionally trying to seduce other men, it's licentious—you are just asking men to come fuck you. Mark my words: if you ever do that, I will break your fucking legs! I'd rather not have a wife than be a cuckold."

Yingzhi had been in such a good mood that morning, and she didn't want to ruin things by arguing with Guiqing. What he said made her shake with anger, but she knew that if she started up with him, things would not come to a good end. Instead, she just cursed him and shouted, "You're crazy!" And then she left the house straightaway without even eating breakfast.

The morning air felt crisp and fresh. The sun hadn't risen yet, and the plains were enveloped in a shroud of expansive morning mist. When the morning wind gently blew, it dispersed the already thin white mist, which disappeared entirely before the sun came up. By the time Yingzhi arrived at Yellow Leaf Swamp, most members of the Sanhuo Band were already there. Yingzhi's old friends from the troupe all joked and exchanged pleasantries for a bit before getting to work on setting up the stage. Wentang was still the DJ. Since it had been a whole year since Yingzhi last sang with the group, Wentang went over the new songs with her. As they were running through the songs, Wentang asked, "Yingzhi, why did you rush off to get married so soon? You didn't even give me a chance to pursue you!"

Yingzhi laughed. "I'm sure you thought a girl like me wasn't up to your standards. You live in town and have a gorgeous wife. I'm just a country girl; I'm in no place to make any demands when it comes to things like marriage."

Wentang also laughed. "For women it doesn't matter if you come from the countryside or the big city. All that matters is if you are pretty, virtuous, and good in bed!"

Yingzhi could feel the spark of something light up inside her. She gazed at Wentang and smiled. "I'm certainly not qualified in the first two categories, but I'm damn good in that last one."

Wentang broke out laughing. "Actually, the first two categories are useless anyway; that last one is the only one that's important. My wife sucks in that category. I wonder if Guiqing can handle you?"

Yingzhi thought about how rough Guiqing was with her in bed and immediately began to shudder, but she said, "I could easily handle another eight Guiqings!" With that she laughed so hard she almost fell down.

As she was laughing, Wentang smirked and said, "Count me in as one of them."

It was as if that comment turned something on between them.

The event at Yellow Leaf Swamp was also a wedding. It was an all-day affair, and the bride wasn't scheduled to arrive until dusk. And so from morning until night the sound of pop songs filled the air surrounding Yellow Leaf Swamp. The Sanhuo Band had four lead singers, and they took turns on stage. Whenever Yingzhi came off the stage to rest between her sets, Wentang would flirt with her. The first time Wentang tried putting his hands on her, Yingzhi slapped him and told him to behave. But instead Wentang just leaned over and whispered in her ear, "You and I both have experience in this department. We'll just have a little fun, but I promise I won't do anything to break up your family." Yingzhi thought what he said made sense. She was already married and her virginity was gone, so what's the harm in having a little fun with him? After thinking about it that way, Yingzhi decided to just let him have his way.

That day at the Yellow Leaf Swamp wedding Yingzhi made 72 yuan. That was a bit less than she used to earn. Sanhuo explained that Yellow Leaf Swamp is a poor place, so they started out with a lower base fee; then, not as many people requested songs, so they made less money than usual. Although Yingzhi was upset that the money she made was on the low side, she decided not to push the matter.

Yingzhi couldn't ride home with the band members because they lived in the opposite direction. She had to walk home alone. She had gone only a few dozen steps when she ran into Wentang, who was coming back from the bathroom. He asked, "You're leaving just like that?"

Yingzhi explained, "If I don't leave now, it will be too late. The rest of them are all loading up the car. What did you sneak off for?"

Wentang didn't say anything; instead, he just grabbed Yingzhi and pulled her toward him. He quickly reached one hand down her pants. Yingzhi struggled for a moment and said, "You're a wicked one, aren't you?"

"I'm just having a little fun," said Wentang.

Yingzhi pushed Wentang away. "And why should I let you have fun with me?"

"Because you turn me on," said Wentang. Just then, the rest of the troupe called for Wentang to help load the car. Wentang removed something from his pocket and slipped it into Yingzhi's hand before grabbing hold of her face and moving in to suddenly suck her lips. He didn't say a word and then turned to run off to join the rest of the band. Yingzhi stood there in shock as she watched his silhouette retreat into the distance. She could feel her heart violently racing. She couldn't help reaching up to touch her lips, for the feeling he left her with was quite unique. Finally, she looked down to see what Wentang had put in her hand. It was a 10 yuan note.

The sky was already dark as Yingzhi made her way home, the whole way thinking about the money she had made. She made 72 yuan singing and an extra 10 for letting Wentang kiss her, for a total of 82 yuan. As far as Yingzhi was concerned, that 10 yuan she got from Wentang was the least work. *From now on I wouldn't go home from a performance with less than 80 yuan in my pocket. If I don't hit that mark, I'll let Wentang have a little fun to make up for that lost cash. It's my body, and I don't need to put up any capital to make money from it. After all, I never got a cent for all the times I let Guiqing fuck me. Besides, I never had a problem with those guys who try to cop a little feel, so why not just go with it? What's more, didn't Wentang say we were just having a little fun? Foreigners are always hugging and kissing each other when they meet; they even do that with strangers. But they consider that good manners. I'll just pretend that I'm abroad showing good manners.*

It was at that point that Yingzhi wondered what she would say if someone else used that logic about foreign manners on her. After thinking about it for a long time, she decided to set up a rule for herself: *As long as they are willing to pay, she is willing to play.* She also came up with a second rule: *They can mess around a bit and flirt as much as they want, but nothing beyond that.* She didn't want to do anything too disrespectful behind her husband's back. That was where Yingzhi's thoughts were when she returned home.

Yingzhi went back to her old life. The amount of money she made gradually started to add up, and she seemed happier by the day. Guiqing didn't have anything to say about Yingzhi's newfound happiness. As far as he was concerned, only those moments in bed when he begged Yingzhi to give him a little cash were important. Although Yingzhi felt annoyed, she realized that keeping him happy was the only way she could continue to go out to sing with the troupe. And as long as she could keep performing, she could keep making money. So whenever Guiqing asked her for money, she would always give him a little.

When the Sanhuo Band went out to perform, they would spend an entire day at each location. When the girls sang, they were always scantily dressed, and they had a lot of contact with the opposite sex, so it was hard to avoid some occasional funny business. Wentang wasn't the only one who fooled around with Yingzhi; some of the other guys in the troupe also got close to her. Another female singer in the band, named Xiaohong, was still single, and she was even more liberal about sex than Yingzhi. Whenever one of the guys in the band asked for a hand with something, Xiaohong would practically shove her body against him. When Yingzhi first saw Xiaohong getting close with Wentang, she was clearly upset. But then Wentang turned around and embraced Yingzhi, saying, "C'mon, we're all just trying to break up the boredom. It's no big deal. Nothing to be jealous about!" Yingzhi thought about it and decided there was indeed no need for her to look at Wentang as her sole property; after all, she didn't belong to him. Later when Zuqiang, one of the male singers, started coming on to her, Yingzhi didn't resist. It wasn't long before everyone in the Sanhuo Band figured out that Xiaohong was willing to go all the way but Yingzhi would stop at fondling and stroking. Xiaohong never asked for money for sex, but you had to pay if you wanted to lay your hands on Yingzhi. All the guys joked that they never imagined that Yingzhi, a married woman, would be in higher demand than Xiaohong, a single girl!

One day the troupe went to Silverwater Village to sing at an old man's funeral. After the banquet the mourners were carrying the coffin out to a small ridge to be buried when it started to rain. The Sanhuo Band ended up stuck in the family's ancestral hall waiting out the downpour. With nothing better to do, the guys in the band started to play poker. Each of them put up 50 yuan, which they handed over to Yingzhi and Xiaohong to split. But in order to keep the money, the girls had to agree to sit on the lap of whoever won as they played their next hand. Sanhuo also joined them. Yingzhi and Xiaohong thought it was a good deal for them, so they spent the game getting passed around to each of the men, who would squeeze and fondle them.

That day Yingzhi made 132 yuan, 50 of which she didn't have to lift a finger to earn. She just had her fun and money came rolling in. She couldn't have been happier.

The rain had stopped by the time she arrived home. Guiqing was lying in bed with a cigarette dangling from his lips and a disgruntled look written all over his face. It took just one glance for Yingzhi to know that he had lost again at the gambling table. She wasn't in the mood to yell at him and instead just reached into her purse and threw him a 20 yuan note.

"Wow, did the sun just rise in the west?" Guiqing exclaimed. "Since when have you given me money without me even having to ask?"

Yingzhi was focused on getting out of her wet clothes and didn't respond to him. Guiqing continued, "Hey Yingzhi, since you are being so generous, why don't you go all the way with it? I'm 50 yuan in the hole with Baldy, I owe 50 yuan to Youjie and another 43 yuan to Fatty. I started out losing today, but then I hit a great winning streak. At first I thought I could make up for my losses, but then Youjie's wife forced him to return home, breaking up the game. Fuck, that fat bitch is going to get what's coming to her one day. Why don't you give me another hundred? Actually, ninety should cover it."

"Keep dreaming. I worked my ass off to make this money while you sit at home. I'm the one supporting you! You not only don't bring home any income but also make us lose money! How does that even make sense?"

"Don't worry, I'll make up for it by taking care of you when you're old. That's fair, right? Anyway, how are you the one supporting me? My parents provide me with food and a roof over my head, and they are more than happy to support me—so I don't see where you come in!"

"You're right. Since your parents are the ones supporting you, why don't you ask them for money?"

"Hey, since my parents are taking care of Jianhuo, shouldn't you give them some money for the baby? So give me the money. I'll pass it on to my mom," demanded Guiqing.

Yingzhi was furious, but then she realized that arguing was useless. She knew that if her relationship with Guiqing blew up, they wouldn't let her out of the house, which would be even worse. Yingzhi threw 90 yuan at Guiqing, yelling, "Let me make it clear: this is the last time! If you need money for clothes, I'll think about giving you some. But I'm not giving you one more cent to pay off your gambling debts."

Guiqing picked up the cash and flipped through the bills before putting on his usual devilish smile. "We'll talk about next time next time. To be honest, I only owe Baldy 20 yuan and You-jie 30. Now I just made an extra 40 yuan; I think I'll buy a bottle of spirits and two packs of cigarettes. That must be okay with you!" With that, he jumped out of bed and went out.

Yingzhi was fuming with anger. She lay in bed thinking about the scene earlier that afternoon when she was getting tossed back and forth between those men. She thought about how their hands were all over her body and suddenly figured, why not let them go a little bit further? As long as they were willing to pay, what was stopping her from sleeping with them? But then on second thought she realized that although the money was enticing, whatever money she might make would be taken by her husband even though it was her body. Letting the whole family spend the money she earned with her body didn't seem fair to her.

That night Yingzhi was so frustrated and confused that she could barely sleep.

VIII

Within the next year Yingzhi had saved more than 1,000 yuan. She hid her bankbook in a place not even Guiqing knew about. Guiqing often tried to find out how much money she had, but she always refused to tell him. On one occasion he was especially vicious and started screaming and cursing at Yingzhi. He said that after marriage all assets between a husband and wife should be shared, so he had every right to know how much money she had in the bank. But Yingzhi talked right back to him: "I'll share my assets with you as soon as you make back that 100 yuan! But as of now, I made all that money, so it's mine." Guiqing argued that one person should earn the money while the other person manages it. Since he was the head of the household, he should be in charge of the money. Yingzhi snapped back that the man of the house should make the money and the woman should manage the money. But right now we have a case of a useless man who is leaving his woman with no choice but to make *and* manage all the money! Guiqing argued that they were no longer living in the old society where men had to go out and be the sole breadwinners. In today's world men and women are equal. If a woman is able to, she should go out and make money; and if a man didn't have the proper skills, he should stay home and manage the money.

The two of them would frequently argue like this over their finances. On one occasion Yingzhi's in-laws even brought in a group of family elders to convene a meeting to settle things on Guiqing's behalf. After the elders heard both sides of the story, they agreed that even if a man is not the main breadwinner, he is still the head of the household and every penny the wife earns should be turned over to her husband. As soon as Guiqing heard the judgment of the elders, he rushed over to Yingzhi to rub it in her face: "Did you hear that? Did you? Listen to what the elders just said! Never in their lives have they heard of a woman being in charge of a family's finances! Men are in charge of the family— that's always been a part of the glorious Chinese tradition!"

Yingzhi knew that she was in a vulnerable position and wasn't sure how to refute what he said, so she just turned to Guiqing and cursed, "Glorious, your ass!"

What Yingzhi said left the elders with a terrible impression of her. But Yingzhi didn't care. As far as she was concerned, they were all part of the same clan, and they were all men; how could she ever expect them to provide a fair judgment of the situation? She earned that money with her own labor and insisted on maintaining full control of it. She was an outsider here. Her in-laws threw obstacles in her way at every turn, while her husband knew only how to eat, drink, and have fun; except for sleeping with her every night, he was completely useless. How could she possibly ever feel comfortable if someone else were controlling her money? And if she gave up that control, what little status she had in the family would be completely gone. The more she thought about it, the more determined she was not to hand that power over to Guiqing. She told him, "Even if you go all the way to Beijing and get the central government to hold a meeting on your behalf, I'm still not handing my money over to you!"

Seeing Yingzhi take such a firm stance left Guiqing utterly beside himself about what to do. He had no choice but to coax Yingzhi into bed when he needed money; later he would warm her up with pillow talk and use his sly charm to coax her into giving him 10 or 20 yuan.

With Yingzhi out making money and his parents taking care of his son, Guiqing didn't have a care in the world. He could spend all his time hanging out and having even more fun with his gang of loser friends.

People in Old Temple Village were a bit different from the residents in other, nearby villages. Most of the able-bodied workers from neighboring villages had all gone south to find work. Most of those villages were made up of people from what Guiqing described as the "386199 brigade." The 38 referred to March 8, which was Women's Day; the 61 referred to June 1, which was Children's Day; and the 99 referred to the Double Ninth Festival on September 9, which celebrates long life and the elderly. When you looked around the neighboring villages, you could barely find a single strong, able-bodied young man.

But for some reason, all the young men in Old Temple Village liked to hang out at home. Residents of Old Temple Village would say that their village wasn't poor and they could afford to support the people who lived there. They'd say, "What is so great about venturing so far away from home anyway? You end up living a tough life in the city and worrying about your parents back at home. What's the point? Chinese people have the old saying 'Knowing contentment leads to long-term happiness.' There is plenty to eat here and you don't have a landlord exploiting you—what could be better than that?" The people of Old Temple Village adopted a philosophy that allowed them to find contentment in simple daily life. They'd say, "That's why the people here have such a tolerant attitude when it comes to young people in their twenties like Guiqing, who just spend all their time relaxing and having fun."

Guiqing was pretty wild when it came to his gambling habits; he would often stay out all night and not return home. The first time he pulled that, Yingzhi was furious. She lay there alone in bed like an empty plot of fertilized land, overgrown with weeds and devoid of songbirds, all alone as the rustling wind quietly whipped by. Later there were several more times when Guiqing stayed out all night, but Yingzhi no longer felt that loneliness. She actually felt more comfortable being alone. The land may have been a barren desert, but deserts can also be beautiful.

Yingzhi's in-laws, on the other hand, were not very happy. No matter what Guiqing did in the village, they never seemed to mind; but his parents put their foot down when it came to his staying out all night. They interpreted Guiqing's behavior not as a sign of their son's gambling addiction but as a sign that Ying-zhi was not taking good enough care of her husband's "needs." They felt that Yingzhi's being out all day working had led Gui-qing to become detached from his family. During dinner they would often make oblique accusations against Yingzhi, which would invariably lead to a full-blown argument. The result was usually Yingzhi's smashing a plate and leaving the table before she even ate.

One time after Guiqing had again stayed out all night, Ying-zhi arose the next morning and, without even bothering to check whether he had come home, got ready and went out to sing with the troupe. When she returned home that evening, the household was in chaos. Her mother-in-law was wailing, and her father-in-law had smashed up a chair and was cursing at the top of his lungs. Having no idea what had happened, Yingzhi immediately asked her sister-in-law, who happened to be home on vacation. She just said, "They're upset about my brother, what else?"

As soon as Yingzhi's father-in-law laid eyes on her, he instantly transferred his anger to her. He yelled, "Where the hell have you been? All you know how to do is run around flirting with those random men, and you don't even bother asking about your own husband!"

After walking in and getting immediately attacked by her father-in-law, Yingzhi lost it. She yelled back, "Who do I flirt with? What are you talking about? Like you are some upstanding father! You open your mouth and immediately start screaming at people!"

Yingzhi's mother-in-law said through her tears, "If something has happened to Guiqing, I'll make you pay!"

"What's happened to Guiqing? Why make me pay? What did I do to him?" yelled Yingzhi.

Seeing everyone screaming at each other, Yingzhi's sister-in-law anxiously tried to calm everyone down. "Stop arguing! My brother's in trouble, but what good is all this arguing going to do him?"

As soon as Yingzhi heard what her sister-in-law said, the color drained from her face and she felt her legs grow weak. She realized that something terrible must have happened to Guiqing for her in-laws to be acting this crazy. What if something really bad happened to him? What if he was dead . . . or injured . . . ? Yingzhi grew scared. She quickly asked, "What happened? What happened to Guiqing?" She could hear her own voice trembling.

Yingzhi's sister-in-law said, "He was arrested last night by the town police."

Yingzhi was in shock. "Arrested? For what?"

Yingzhi's sister-in-law lowered her voice. "According to You-jie's wife, they were at the Hot Girls Dance Club in town . . . they said that they . . . they . . ."

Although her heart dropped and a feeling of disgust welled up inside her, Yingzhi insisted on hearing it, so she pushed her sister-in-law. "What did they do?"

Yingzhi's sister-in-law looked upset but impatiently continued, "It's terrible. What my brother did is so disgusting . . . they gang-raped one of the girls who works at the club."

Yingzhi felt as if her anger were bursting through her chest. She jumped to her feet and screamed at her in-laws, "This is that great son of yours! And you have the gall to yell at *me* instead of him! He goes out and acts like a hooligan. As your daughter-in-law, I'm the one being shamed here!"

But Yingzhi's mother-in-law was not going to stand by and take that. "Guiqing was a great kid before he married you," she yelled. "He never once got into trouble. He was well behaved and always respected his parents. But ever since he married you, he doesn't even bother coming home anymore!"

Yingzhi's father-in-law was even more unbridled in his attack. "Guiqing left his wife at home to go screw around with some other woman. And you claim that isn't your fault! It's your job to keep him happy. If you had done your job, how would he have the energy to go out screwing around like that? If my son picks up some dirty STD out there, I will hold you 100 percent responsible!"

All the anger and sadness Yingzhi had pent up came to the surface. She thought about how hard she worked to make money, often leaving early and coming home late. Sometimes she would leave the house without eating breakfast, and by the time she came home only a few scraps of food would be left from dinner for her to eat. Meanwhile, Guiqing ate his fill and sat on his ass every day with nothing to do. As if drinking and gambling weren't enough, he even cheated on her by going out and fooling around with those disgusting prostitutes! What was the point of even staying married to a man so lowly and depraved? Just thinking about it compounded her unhappiness, and Yingzhi broke down in a fit of uncontrollable tears. She had no interest in arguing with her in-laws or asking her sister-in-law any more questions, nor did she want to go to the police station to find out what really happened; she didn't even consider using her connections to try to get Guiqing out of jail. She was a complete blank. She simply entered her bedroom in tears and collapsed onto the bed. Her only wish was to die right then and there.

Guiqing came home the following day around noon. He looked disgruntled, as if his whole body had been covered in a layer of frost. It was as if someone had stripped him of that air of lively arrogance that normally characterized him. As far as he was concerned, what happened yesterday had been the worst night of his life. He usually just went to the nightclub to sing some karaoke and have a little fun, but then Fatty and the others decided to call in some prostitutes. He was afraid that Yingzhi would be upset if she found out, he said, so he made sure not to join in; he just sat off to one side of the room singing his songs. Who could have imagined that the police would show up and take him down to the station along with the others? He spent the entire night enduring their interrogations, insults, beatings, and curses—they didn't even treat him like a human being. Finally, just before dawn they got to the bottom of what happened; they decided that he didn't really do anything wrong and released him. Never in his life had Guiqing felt so wronged.

Guiqing's parents greeted him with celebratory joy. They passed him a basin of water to wash his face with and brought him a cup of tea and food. It was as if he had just returned in glory from a long trip. Having been up all night, Yingzhi put her ear against the door when she heard the commotion coming from the living room and knew that Guiqing had returned. Although she absolutely despised him, she heaved a sigh of relief that he was home safely.

Guiqing wiped his face, but he wasn't in the mood to talk to his parents; instead, he just lowered his head and asked, "Where's Yingzhi?"

Guiqing's father-in-law said, "We argued all night. Your mother and I were so upset we couldn't sleep."

"Let me go explain to her what happened," Guiqing said.

But Guiqing's mother said, "What happened was no big deal, and she made a fuss about it all night! Instead of trying to get her man out of jail, all she did was focus on how wronged she was! What's there to explain to her?"

Guiqing was clearly annoyed. "She's my wife. If I don't tell her the truth about what happened, who am I supposed to tell?"

But Guiqing's mother continued, "Back in the old days all the rich men had three wives and six concubines! Sure, we are now living in the new society, but what's the big deal if a man fools around a little? Is that something worth staying up all night crying about?"

Guiqing responded, "Can you two please just stop it! I didn't fool around!"

"What? You didn't do anything wrong? Then why the hell do you think the police arrested you?" Guiqing's father yelled.

"The other guys were the ones messing with that girl. I was just there in the room singing when everything went down. So when the police showed up, they naturally arrested everyone in the room," Guiqing explained.

Guiqing's mother immediately raised her voice and started yelling so that Yingzhi could hear, "Did you hear that! My son didn't do anything wrong! You're the one who doesn't believe what your own husband says! So what are you crying about!"

Yingzhi could hear everything they were talking about loud and clear. Just hearing the tone of voice her in-laws were using made her furious. In her anger, Yingzhi threw on her clothes. Her disheveled hair was matted to her face, and her swollen eyes looked like a pair of engorged peaches. In just one night, the gorgeous and alluring Yingzhi had transformed into a different person. Guiqing couldn't help feeling bad when he saw her. He figured, no matter what anyone said, he knew he had made a mistake . . . and he knew that those tears on Yingzhi's face had been shed for him.

When Yingzhi stormed out of her room, she didn't even glance at Guiqing but instead charged at her mother-in-law, screaming with a wicked tone, "And what if I cried? Don't tell me that if your man went out and fucked someone else's wife, you would start singing songs about how wonderfully talented he was!"

This sudden attack took Yingzhi's mother-in-law completely off guard. She just stood there speechless. It took her a few seconds to process what had just happened, and then she turned white with anger. She slapped her thigh and roared, "Would you listen to that? Is that how a daughter-in-law is supposed to speak to her mother-in-law? Do you realize that when you talk about 'my man,' you are referring to your own father-in-law? Guiqing, you heard what she just said. That's the kind of evil I have to put up with every day with her! She even has the gall to curse your parents right in front of you!"

"All I said was one sentence and look at the way you're barking! Don't tell me I'm not allowed to cry when my man runs off and fucks prostitutes!"

Guiqing's father was so angry that he began to shake; even the tone of his voice began to change. He pointed to Guiqing's nose. "Don't tell me you're not going to slap this evil bitch!"

Yingzhi strutted up to Guiqing and looked him in the eye. Raising her head and extending her chest, she screamed, "That's right, hit me! Go ahead! You screw with those sluts outside and come home to beat your wife—now that's a real man!"

When Guiqing first saw his wife's swollen eyes after she had been crying all night, he actually felt quite sorry for her. Even though he had spent the whole night filled with anger, he did feel at least a little bit guilty about what he had done. He had initially planned to come home to console his wife, but after seeing Yingzhi cause such a scene, his pity, his guilt, and any urge to console her all went out the window. He thought, *Fuck, I think I have no choice but to educate this bitch! One little hiccup like this and she turned our entire family upside down. What would she do if something serious happened? Kill my parents?* With that thought, Guiqing raised his hand and gave Yingzhi, who was already right there in his face, a wicked slap across the cheek. He hit her so hard that she stumbled backward several steps. Yingzhi clasped her cheek in shock at the completely unexpected blow and stared blankly at Guiqing for several minutes. The look in her eyes expressed shock and confusion.

When she realized what had just happened, Yingzhi was brimming with a mix of sadness and anger. Like an angry lioness, she extended her arms and hurled herself at Guiqing, howling and screaming at him. Now it was Quiqing's turn to be taken by surprise. He didn't have time to get out of the way or put up a defense, and before he realized what was happening, he had three bloody scratches on his face from Yingzhi's nails. Guiqing tried to push Yingzhi off with one hand as he held his face with the other. Blood was oozing from Guiqing's face, dripping into the palm of his hand. When he caught sight of the blood, it was as if someone had added oil to the flames of his anger, which was now at the boiling point. He grabbed Yingzhi with both hands and lifted his right leg to kick her in the stomach. Yingzhi screamed, releasing her grip on Guiqing and then curling up on the floor. But Yingzhi's scream did little to quell her husband's anger. He lifted his leg a second time and kicked her in the ass. Yingzhi was already on the ground and had no way to resist or protect herself. Guiqing continued hitting her and stomping on her, all the while cursing, "You dare to raise your hand to me! You think you are the police! You want to treat me like an animal too? I'll fucking kill you! Let's see if you ever again dare to get out of line in this house!"

Yingzhi rolled around on the floor howling in pain, but she didn't dare curse him anymore. All this happened in the living room, where displayed on the wall was a portrait of the political leader and, just above it, were five words written in bold calligraphy: *Heaven, Earth, Ruler, Parents, Teacher.* Yingzhi's father-in-law had personally written those characters with a brush. Beneath the portrait and calligraphy was a dark brown table with much of its paint already peeling. Yingzhi's in-laws sat down on either side of that table and coldly looked down at Yingzhi as she squirmed on the floor moaning in pain.

IX

The day she was beaten, a sad and angry Yingzhi went home to her parents. It happened to be the slow season, so there wasn't any work to be done in the fields; Yingzhi's father was keeping an eye on their shop while her brothers and sisters-in-law were both sitting around the table playing mah-jongg. Yingzhi's mother, who was out in the pigpen feeding the animals, called out to Yingzhi, "It's not a holiday, what brings you back home? How come you didn't bring Jianhuo along with you?" Yingzhi was too embarrassed to tell them about the beating; she wouldn't have any face left if she told them. She instead just said that Old Temple Village was boring and she missed her parents, so she came back to see them. One of Yingzhi's sisters-in-law was in the middle of mixing the mah-jongg tiles, which made a swooshing sound. She laughed as she said, "Ha, I never took you for the filial type!" Yingzhi's sister-in-law felt no ill will and was just trying to make a lighthearted joke, but the comment didn't sit well with Yingzhi.

As they were having dinner, Yingzhi's sister-in-law asked Yingzhi to play mah-jongg, but Yingzhi wasn't in the mood and found an excuse to decline. As Yingzhi stepped outside, she was feeling depressed and decided to take a walk around the village.

A few people in the village said hello when they saw her walking. There were even a few kids who followed her imitating her singing. It had been so long since she had spent time in the village that the neighbors' dogs no longer recognized her and started barking as she walked by. Everything about the village left Yingzhi with a warm and familiar feeling. Old Temple Village, by contrast, felt more and more like hell. Yingzhi wondered why she had to get married off to such a hellish place.

Without realizing it, Yingzhi ended up outside Sanhuo's house. Sanhuo had the best house in the entire village. It was three stories tall, and the most amazing thing about his house was that every bedroom had its own bathroom. For a time, there was a joke going around the village that Sanhuo spent a fortune and pulled out all the stops to build the largest bathroom anyone had seen. They said, "If you want to take a shit, all you need is a makeshift outhouse, so why do you need all that fancy stuff?" But Sanhuo just yelled at them, "What the hell do you know!"

Yingzhi understood that only someone with Sanhuo's knowledge and drive could understand how to make our short lives as comfortable as possible. It was thanks to Sanhuo that his family was able to live a proud and carefree lifestyle. It was a pity that Guiqing wasn't even half the man that Sanhuo was.

She could hear Sanhuo's laughter and giggles coming from upstairs as he played with his grandchildren. It was a joyous sound that showed no trace of sadness. Yingzhi looked up and could see the light in the window upstairs. The bright glow was especially eye-catching as it cut through the darkness.

As if that light all at once turned something on inside her, Yingzhi wondered, *Even though I'm a woman, what's stopping me from achieving the same things that Sanhuo has? Why do I have to be stuck living with my in-laws and dealing with their insults every day? If I save up enough money, why can't I build a house for myself like Sanhuo? They always say that building a house is the kind of thing men do, but if a woman is capable, why can't she do it too? I can make a few hundred yuan a month—that's several thousand each year. I should be able to have enough to build a house in less than two years. There's no reason I need a three-story house like Sanhuo's; two stories should be enough. I could live upstairs and look down on my in-laws' courtyard. I wouldn't have to care about them cursing me or deal with their moody bullshit. I could just kick my feet up and ignore them, and whenever I feel like it, I could even spit down at them. How great would that be?*

This new idea excited Yingzhi. All night long she couldn't get the image of that new house out of her mind. She imagined all the types of pretty houses she could think of and went through them one by one. She realized that the appearance of this new house would completely transform her entire life. Even when the sun came up the next morning, she was still excited by the idea. Yingzhi thought, *Guiqing, go ahead and keep having your fun, keep sitting on your ass; do whatever the hell you want. I'll show you! I may be a woman, I may be someone's wife, someone's daughter-in-law, but none of that is going to stop me from building my own house! I'll use that house to make you all turn red with jealousy and anger, and I'll laugh at you!*

That morning as Yingzhi was having breakfast, Guiqing showed up on his bicycle to pick his wife up. Yingzhi was still consumed with thoughts of her new house, and most of the anger from the insult of the other day had abated. When Guiqing saw that Yingzhi seemed to be in a decent mood, he silently heaved a sigh of relief. He was planning on putting on a smile and apologizing to Yingzhi for his behavior, but before he could even open his mouth, he saw her flash him a wink—and he immediately understood that she hadn't told her family about what happened. He could now let go of those worries that had been consuming him since Yingzhi left. Relieved, Guiqing put on his old naughty face and said, "What do you say? Have you had enough fun? I came to take you home?"

Yingzhi's sister-in-law laughed. "My oh my, Guiqing! You are like a little bell tied to your wife's leg! Our dear Yingzhi has been home only for a day, and your little bell is already ringing to take her home!"

Guiqing chuckled, then said, "I could never get away with being so useless if it wasn't for my wife! We rely on Yingzhi for everything! I can't live a normal human life without her!"

Everyone at the breakfast table broke out in laughter. Her parents' laughter was filled with pride for their daughter. Yingzhi said nothing as they laughed but just bid farewell to her family and rode off with Guiqing.

Yingzhi sat on the back of Guiqing's bike, but neither of them spoke. As they passed the spot by the river where they had first had sex, Yingzhi hopped off the bike and sat down in the grass as if upset. Guiqing could tell that she was about to blow her fuse again, so he quickly set the bike down and sat down next to her and said, "Yingzhi, please don't be angry. I was in such a bad mood last night. The whole thing with the prostitute had nothing to do with me—it was all Youjie and Fatty! Because of them I ended up spending an entire night at the police station. I was so upset. When I finally got home, all I wanted to do was rest, but then you and my parents got into that big fight. I was so frustrated that I just lost it. Otherwise, how could I ever have hit you like that? When did I ever do anything like that? Why don't I let you hit me back? I promise I won't lift a finger to defend myself."

Hearing Guiqing speak brought all those feelings of being wronged back to Yingzhi; she started to cry. Guiqing repeatedly apologized, but Yingzhi just kept quietly sobbing. Realizing that repeating the same things wasn't going to help, Guiqing shut his mouth; he just sat there beside her looking depressed. He was chewing on a piece of grass as he gazed out into the distance as if in a trance.

Yingzhi had cried enough. She knew that tears were of no use. She wiped the tears from her face and said, "I'll forgive you on one condition: I don't want to live under the same roof as your parents."

Guiqing was taken aback. "If we don't live with my parents, then where are we going to live? You don't want me to be a live-in son-in-law, do you?"

"We'll build our own house and live on our own," said Yingzhi.

"Us? Where would we even build a house?" asked Guiqing.

"I know about that empty plot of land beside your house. We could build it there," suggested Yingzhi. "As long as the two of us are on the same page, I can work hard to make money, you can borrow a bit from your parents, and we should be able to build a house in the next year or so. At our age we should have a place of our own. What's the point of you going on wasting away your time like you've been doing? If you keep on like this, you'll have nothing left? Wouldn't it be better to go out and make some money?"

"I don't object to making money. I've got a friend in the county seat who is a contractor that does renovations. He does pretty good for himself. A few days ago he even sent someone over to see if I would be willing to help out. I could even go there tomorrow. But I don't see why we have to build our own house. We've got more than enough rooms in our current house. Even if I were to take a few more wives, we'd still have enough room! So why waste all that money building a new house? Besides, how many sons and daughters-in-law do you know that don't live with their parents?" explained Guiqing.

"You're really hopeless!" sighed Yingzhi. "What's so bad about us living our own independent life?"

"It would be breaking up the family!" argued Guiqing. "The villagers would all laugh at us, and I'm afraid my parents would refuse to go along with this."

Yingzhi became upset. "Are you married to your parents or me?"

"My parents are old and I'm their only son. We'll be able to live on our own after they are gone. Why should we expend so much energy building a new house? Think about it, it's just not worth the trouble," argued Guiqing.

Yingzhi flashed a cold smile. "Seeing how much energy your parents have, I'm afraid that they'll outlive me! So I'll make it simple for you: Are you in or not? If not, let's just get a divorce!"

Guiqing was taken completely off guard by her ultimatum. "Don't say such things! You wouldn't want to deprive Jianhuo of his mother! Besides, without someone to look after my needs at night, you'll be practically forcing me to go out to hook up with random women!" As Guiqing spoke, he flashed that arrogant smile of his and reached out to caress Yingzhi.

Yingzhi pushed him away, saying, "If you agree with my plan, I'll continue living at your parents' house for the time being. I can stand one more year, but eventually I need a lifeline, which will be having our own house."

Guiqing sighed and said, "You're being so dramatic; you sound like you're about to die or something! What the hell, fine, I'll go along with your plan. Anyway, you and my parents are like oil and water. I'll talk it over with my parents after I get home. Are you happy now?"

Yingzhi didn't say anything, but she was pleased with Guiqing's attitude.

Everything turned out to be much smoother than Yingzhi had ever imagined. A lot of that came down to the fact that Guiqing was such a smooth talker. Guiqing said, "If we build our own house, I'll go out and get a real job to make some extra money; that'll also give me a direction in life. But if you don't let us build our own house, I'll just continue making trouble with Youjie, Baldy, Fatty, and the rest of those guys. Who knows, I might even end up getting arrested again!"

When Yingzhi's in-laws first heard about their wanting to build their own house, they both grew sullen and started shouting. Her father-in-law was in the living room and her mother-in-law was in the kitchen, and they both were yelling at Guiqing at the same time. They both knew it must have been Yingzhi's idea. Even though neither of them could stand the sight of their daughter-in-law, they weren't willing to agree. Privately, they said there was no way they were going to let the slut get her way.

But after hearing what Guiqing said, they saw the logic in his words. His recent arrest had already been too much of a shock for them. After Youjie, Fatty, and Baldy were released on bail, they all stayed in bed for three full days. When they finally dragged themselves out of bed, they all trembled when they talked about how badly the police had beaten them. Guiqing was lucky: although he told everyone that he had no interest in the girl, Youjie and the others told everyone that the only reason he got off was because the police came before it was his turn with the girl. If such a thing were to happen again and Guiqing ended up beaten by the police, things would be much worse. When they thought about it like that, Guiqing's parents decided that maybe it was a good idea for him to go out and get a job. If they built their new house right next door, it would be as if they never left.

After talking it over, Yingzhi's in-laws agreed to their request. They raised just two conditions: First, the courtyards for the two houses should be connected with a gate so that Guiqing and Jianhuo could easily go back and forth. And second, Guiqing and Yingzhi needed to pay for the construction on their own.

When Guiqing told Yingzhi what they said, she immediately agreed to the first condition, which would also be convenient for her. But she drew a long face as soon as she heard the second condition and began to curse her in-laws. Guiqing interrupted, "Yingzhi, you know you're cursing my parents, right? This is like cursing me! Do you agree to what they said? If not, I'll go talk to them again. Anyway, it's not like *I* want to build a new house. I'm only doing this for you."

Yingzhi clenched her teeth and thought about it again. At first she was going to yell at Guiqing, but on second thought she realized that she would only be alienating her husband. She needed him to be on her side. If this plan should blow up, she would be even worse off. Perhaps it was better to just accept it. She swallowed her anger and said, "If they're not willing to contribute to the new house, so be it! I'll go out and make the money we need. I know I'll be able to earn enough to build a house."

That night at dinner Yingzhi wore a smug look that really got under the skin of her mother-in-law. As she ate, Yingzhi's mother-in-law said, "I'm doing this for my son. If it wasn't for him, I'd never agree to let my land be used to build a new house." Yingzhi's mother-in-law raised her voice so that Yingzhi would be sure to hear her every word. Yingzhi surreptitiously sneered and thought, *I don't give a shit who you're doing this for, just as long as you stay true to your word and allow us to build that house.*

X

The next morning Guiqing really did head off to the county seat to start his new job. He returned after a few days complaining about how pathetically low the pay was for all the exhausting work involved. Yingzhi's mother-in-law quickly said, "If it's too much for you, why don't you take a few days off to rest at home?" Guiqing took her up on the suggestion and stayed on at the village. The first thing he did was go out to play mah-jongg; he returned in the middle of the night and then ended up having a long tryst with Yingzhi. By the time he finally lay down to sleep, it was almost dawn and he was completely exhausted. He ended up spending that entire day in bed. On the third day after he got home, Yingzhi woke him up first thing to go back to work, but Guiqing just lay in bed stretching. It was only after Yingzhi kept prodding him until she almost lost her temper that he finally listlessly crawled out of bed. He kept going on about how going to work was to ensure a comfortable future for them; not working was to enjoy comfortable life today. Either way he was going to have a comfortable life, so why not just live for today? Yingzhi sneered at Guiqing: He was already in his twenties—how could he possibly be so immature?

In order to get Guiqing out the door, Yingzhi had to calm down and patiently persuade him how important it was for him to go back to work. He finally left, but he looked utterly disinterested in going. Yingzhi's mother-in-law was sorry to see him go; as they ate breakfast, she kept telling him not to go if he didn't want to and no one should force him to do anything he didn't want to. Guiqing shot a glance at Yingzhi; he didn't respond to his mother's suggestion. As Guiqing left, his mother stood at the front door gazing sorrowfully at her departing son. Yingzhi felt quite proud, though; it was as if she had finally won a battle. She thought, *Now that your son's married, don't expect him to still listen to everything you say.*

But he wasn't gone long . . . Guiqing was back before dinner. His arm was wrapped in a white bandage, but his face had a rosy glow. Yingzhi anxiously asked him what happened. Guiqing explained that as he was putting ceramic tile up on a wall, one of the other guys cut the next piece of tile and tried to hand it to him; but Guiqing didn't notice, and when he turned around the tile sliced his arm, taking off a big chunk of flesh. "All of a sudden my arm was bleeding like a river!"

When Guiqing spoke he always liked to exaggerate. Yingzhi knew there was no way his injury was as serious as he had described it; she pursed her lips as a sign of disdain. Her mother-in-law, on the other hand, immediately started to scream, "Oh my poor son! It is terrible to lose so much blood! Yingzhi, what are you standing there for? Hurry up and help your man to the bed! You should rush out and buy some cubes of coagulated pig's blood to replenish the blood he lost! Did you break any bones? Yingzhi, hurry up and get him some spare ribs!"

One of the things Yingzhi despised most was when her mother-in-law got into this kind of mood. So Yingzhi decided to just stand there coldly staring at her mother-in-law. Finally, she turned to Guiqing and said, "Wow, judging from your mother's reaction, one would think that you were half dead!"

"That's because my mother cares! Look at you! Your husband is lying here hurt and you don't even raise an eyebrow!" complained Guiqing.

"How should I know how bad your injury really is? You got a little cut and lost a few drops of blood. Big deal! I don't see that injury impeding you from eating, drinking, pissing, or shitting! Hell, the other day I was sewing a button on a pair of shorts and poked my hand, but you didn't hear me whine about it!"

Guiqing was geting upset. "So you think I'm pretending to be injured just so I can get out of work?"

Yingzhi thought, *Don't tell me you're not?* She flashed him a cold smirk. "You said it, not me!"

"That's right, you didn't say a word. But I know exactly what you're thinking, you cold-hearted bitch!" Guiqing was fuming.

All the while Guiqing's father-in-law had been silent, but now he joined in. "Your husband is hurt like this and you have the nerve to put on a long face and argue with him? Why are you even still here? Go buy the stuff your mother-in-law asked you to get!"

Her father-in-law's words only upset her more. She even thought, *What's he going to do if I don't go? Now they want me to buy pig's blood and ribs. Well, who's going to pay for all that? He doesn't earn a single penny and just relies completely on my money to support him. Keep dreaming!* As Yingzhi went through all that in her mind, she snorted a "humph" and, without a word, turned around and went into her bedroom. She lay down on the bed and intentionally started humming a song just to annoy them.

Before she could finish her song, Guiqing barged into the room. His hand was grasping a leather belt; he made a "humph" sound just as Yingzhi had and, without saying a word, started to whip her. Taken off guard, Yingzhi screamed and tried to get up to reason with Guiqing. But as soon as she lifted her body, the belt came down on her face. Yingzhi could feel the burning pain on her cheek. Her screams turned into tearful wails. Guiqing completely ignored her cries and just kept violently whipping her. Yingzhi used the pillow to cover her face, and her voice reduced to a trembling whimper, like the cries of a wounded wolf. Yingzhi's heart was in so much pain, but then she heard her son, Jianhuo, giggling outside the door. Yingzhi's mother-in-law complimented the baby: "What a good boy! When our little Jianhuo grows up, he'll be just like his daddy. He won't let anybody take advantage of him! Whoever bullies you will get a whipping!" Yingzhi silently cursed them, thinking, *One day, I'm going to kill you all!*

Guiqing eventually ran out of energy and threw the belt on to the bed. He said, "I'll keep beating you until you learn how to start behaving like a proper wife!"

With those words, Guiqing walked out, and the room suddenly fell silent. The only remaining sound was Yingzhi's sobbing. Exhausted from crying, she too finally fell silent. She tried to pull herself up, but as soon as she moved, her entire body was in pain. More tears gushed out. The more she thought about what had happened, the stronger a suffocating feeling became. She didn't think she had wronged her husband and couldn't understand why he was so cruel. She looked up at the wedding photo hanging on the wall; in it she was all made up and Guiqing was gazing at her with a big open smile. He looked as if he couldn't have been happier in that photo. And now that same man who was once so happy had beaten her within an inch of her life. *How can men be such beasts?* Yingzhi suddenly thought how terribly difficult her life had become. It was something she never before imagined could happen.

Guiqing stayed out all night gambling and didn't return until the next morning. When he walked in the door, he ordered Yingzhi, "Bring me a basin of hot water to wash up!"

Yingzhi was about to talk back to him, but when she thought about the whipping from the previous night and the fact that her body was still sore, she held her tongue. She brought the basin to the kitchen to fill it up with hot water and carried it over to him. She had injuries on her arms, her thighs, and all over her back. Her clothing rubbing against her skin hurt so much she wanted to scream. But what would be the point of screaming? Yingzhi had no choice but to bear it all.

Guiqing washed his face, let out a long yawn, and motioned for Yingzhi to dump out the water. As he climbed into bed, he said, "I guess this is the only way to get you to behave."

Yingzhi didn't respond, but inside she was cursing him: *Fuck your mother!*

After that, Guiqing stopped going into the city for work. Yingzhi also gave up on asking him to find a job. Instead, Guiqing spent all his time in the village gambling; every so often he would go out to the orchard for a day or two to help out his dad. He was quite happy with his life. At night he would try to humor Yingzhi to keep her happy. But Yingzhi no longer asked him to do anything. All she thought about was how she could build that house as quickly as possible so that she could get away from her in-laws and live her own life. She went out to the county seat several times just to check out the type of construction used on the houses there. She made sketches of all the houses she liked there. She even made a few trips to the brick factory; a few friends had helped introduce her to the head of the factory so that she could try to get a good price on bricks for her new house. She also visited the cement factory; her second brother had an old classmate who worked there in shipment—he promised to help her purchase cement at the discount factory price. She even visited all the ceramic tile stores in the county; after comparing them all, she finally settled on a store with affordable and good-looking tiles. She knew that Sanhuo's house had a tile floor, and she wanted her home to be just as beautiful as his. And it had to have an indoor bathroom. Every day she busied herself looking at these stores and factories. She kept thinking, *I may be a woman, but I'm still going to build a house for all of you to see!* Yingzhi had her own goal in life, and she tried to just ignore the way her in-laws and Guiqing looked at her.

In the blink of an eye, it was Chinese New Year again. The Spring Festival holiday was always the busiest time of year for the Sanhuo Band. It's unclear why, but there were always tons of people getting married and a lot of people dying during those months. The Sanhuo Band had a string of bookings, with performances virtually every day or two. Sanhuo had a telephone installed in his house, and it was constantly ringing. Everyone in the village quickly became familiar with that sound. Every time the phone rang, someone in the village would say, "Another idiot is getting ready to send that motherfucker Sanhuo some cash!"

But Yingzhi couldn't wait for that phone to ring; that sound was like music to her ears because it meant she would be able to make more money. Yingzhi used to head over to the agricultural bank every so often to deposit the money she had earned singing, but these days she was so busy performing that she didn't even have time to make a trip to the bank. Instead of trying to get to the bank, she sewed a few secret pockets into her cotton jacket and hid the money in there. There were a few times when she was lying in bed and saw Guiing going through her pockets, but she just pretended not to notice. Her money was her own, and no way was she going to hand it over to Guiqing. She knew that the second her money fell into his hands, it would be gone.

Even if he had only a single dollar to his name, he would use that money to buy alcohol or cigarettes, or he would gamble it away. She refused to let Guiqing waste her money like that. Money should be spent on the things money was meant for, like building a house.

It started to snow again, and the end of the year was almost here. Someone named Liu San hired the Sanhuo Band to perform at Wild Goose Village. Liu San had gone down to Guangdong for work and made a ton of money; he returned home in glory and insisted on hiring the Sanhuo Band to perform a special concert for the entire village. He wanted to host a big party as a way of thanking everyone for taking care of his parents while he had been away. Just before the performance started, Liu San engaged in some small talk with Sanhuo and Yingzhi. When he learned they were from Phoenix Dike, he immediately asked them if they knew a girl named Chunhui. Yingzhi replied, "Of course! She was my classmate—the most useless person in the world!" He was shocked to hear that. "How is that possible? If she's useless, then I don't know who's useful in this world! Her computer skills are amazing; she got offered a job from a big company before she even graduated from college. During summer break she would drive to work in her own car. She was really something! At one point, we had a get-together with a bunch of people from our home province and invited her—and she ended up treating us! That meal ended up costing her more than 1,000 yuan, but she didn't even blink as she paid the bill." Yingzhi listened in shock. She never imagined that Chunhui, who couldn't even walk alone at night without someone guiding her, would end up doing so well for herself. Sanhuo noticed her reaction and said, "What's there to compare? She's a university graduate. Knowledge opens up doors. Everyone has their own fate in life."

For the very first time Yingzhi thought that maybe skipping college wasn't such a good idea.

Since it was snowing, the band set up for their special concert inside the Liu family's ancestral hall. The stage in the hall was from back when they used to perform flower-drum opera there; behind the stage was a small changing room for the actors to put on their costumes and apply their makeup.

The sound quality inside the hall was much better than that of their regular outdoor shows. Yingzhi and Xiaohong hit the stage in a set of skimpy costumes that showed off their arms and backs. They put everything into their performance, earning a wave of thunderous applause after every song. The ancestral hall was packed with people and seething with activity. But it was still winter, and every time Yingzhi and Xiaohong got on or off the stage, they were freezing. There was a coal heater in the back changing room, so as soon as they stepped offstage, they would scurry into that little room to warm up.

About halfway through the performance the atmosphere in the room was really on fire. Work was light during the winter months for most of the people in the village, and those who had left to work in the cities were all home for Chinese New Year. People were usually quite bored and idle during this time of year; the concert was a rare chance for everyone to get together and have fun. The ancestral hall was completely packed with people. Some of the villagers who had returned home after having spent time in the south had more liberal tastes and thought the kind of music being performed was out of fashion. To spice things up a bit, they started calling out to the stage. The first one to call out like that was Liu San. He yelled, "Hey, aren't you wearing too much?" His voice wasn't that loud, but it cut through the room like a bolt of lightning. People immediately started to echo his calls. Amid the chaos, it didn't take long before their calls were reduced to a simple chant: "Strip! Strip! Strip!"

At that moment it was Xiaohong on stage. At first she couldn't tell what they were screaming. She just reprimanded the audience in a coquettish tone. But once she figured out what they were actually chanting, she froze. She turned to look at her boss, Sanhuo, for direction. Seeing how the situation was changing, he quicky went over to pull Liu San aside. Liu San said, "If the girls go topless, I'll give them each a 200 yuan tip. If they strip butt naked, I'll give them 500 each! But that deal's only for the girls, not the guys! There's nothing those guys have worth seeing!" Sanhuo heard that rate and, after calculating how much his cut would be, he immediately agreed.

As soon as Xiaohong came off the stage, Sanhuo told her about the offer. Xiaohong put a jacket over her shoulders and her face was flushed. She sat down next to the heater and thought about it. She said, "It's not easy to make 500 yuan. If he wants me to strip, I'll do it. Anyway, it's not like I know any of these people. Yingzhi, what about you?"

The temptation of making a quick-and-easy 500 yuan made her heart race. She figured if she could make that kind of money at each performance, she would have enough to build her house in no time. But then she thought about what it would really be like to strip in front of all those people, and a bloodcurdling sensation assaulted her.

Yingzhi hesitated. "I'm afraid I can't do it. I'm married . . . if my husband were to find out, he'd kill me."

But Xiaohong argued, "Would he still kill you if he got a cut of the money? Just offer him 200, and I'll bet he won't dare to lay a finger on you!"

"You're right . . ." replied Yingzhi. "But all these villages are nearby; if my parents should ever hear about it, I'd have no dignity left."

"In our village all the women are always pulling out their breasts in front of people when they breastfeed and no one ever says a thing! If you can show them a little skin and make 200 yuan, what's wrong with that? All we're showing off is the beauty of the human body."

Yingzhi was still hesitating, but Xiaohong continued, "Anyway, I'm not scared. Number one, I'm not from around here. Number two, I have no plans to stay here long term. Sooner or later I'm heading to Guangdong to find work. So I'll take the money!"

Yingzhi was going through a fierce mental debate about what to do, but in the end she couldn't get the thought of that 500 yuan out of her head. If she could make 500 for each performance, she would be able to start construction on her new house in less than six months. But . . . when Yingzhi thought about it from the other side of things, she couldn't help feeling somewhat depressed. She was different than Xiaohong: Xiaohong was single and could go wherever she wanted; there was no one relying on her. But Yingzhi was someone's wife; she was a mother to Jianhuo. Everything she did had an impact on other people. Moreover, she had grown up in this area; she knew that once her family heard the rumors, they'd never let her live this down. How could she possibly get naked in front of all those people? How could she ever stand for people gossiping about her behind her back? Yingzhi kept going back and forth but couldn't make up her mind.

Xiaohong had already hit the stage and the music was raging. Every syllable that Xiaohong sang was like a hammer pounding on Yingzhi's heart. The audience couldn't have been more

excited; the room was filled with people hollering and screaming. Yingzhi could tell that Xiaohong had already starting taking
her clothes off. In the end, with every single person in the audience screaming, it sounded like a series of bombs exploding. It
felt as if the roof were going to be blown off the building and go
straight up into the sky.

But Yingzhi still wasn't ready to go out to watch. She just
sat there alone in the back room beside the heater. Her sadness
struck a strange contrast with the excitement just outside the
door. As she gazed into the flames from the heater, she could
almost see the image of Chunhui wearing a fashionable outfit
and driving straight toward her. What right did a useless girl like
Chunhui have to do so well in life? Would Yingzhi have been
able to do even better than Chunhui if she had gone south to
seek out opportunities there? She realized then that all her problems came from her marriage to Guiqing.

When Xiaohong finally finished her set, she wrapped herself in a jacket and rushed back into the dressing room. She was
so cold that her lips were blue, but she was so excited that her
face had a red glow. Somewhat shocked, Yingzhi had never seen
Xiaohong look so beautiful. Sanhuo followed Xiaohong into the
dressing room and told her, "Xiaohong, you were amazing! You
earned that 500! Yingzhi, you didn't see the scene out there! I've
been all over the place these years, but even I have never seen
anything like that! The excitement coming from the audience
really set Xiaohong on fire!"

"I didn't even feel cold," said Xiaohong. "It was so fucking
exciting! Yingzhi, why don't you give it a try?"

The next one up after Xiaohong was Yingzhi. As Yingzhi
ascended to the stage, the audience was still in high spirits from
Xiaohong's performance. Before Yingzhi even started singing,
someone yelled, "Keep the show going! Take it off!"

Yingzhi didn't respond but just smiled. And she began to sing when the music started. But nobody was really paying attention to what she was singing; instead, the audience were in a hub-bub. Wave after wave of cries broke out shouting "Strip!" as if they were all waiting to see Yingzhi take off her clothes. She got through the first half of her song but still hadn't done any-thing that indicated she was going to strip. Some of the audience members became impatient, yelling, "If you're not gonna strip, then get the hell off the stage!" and "Bring up the next one!"

Sitting in the front row was Liu San; he took out five bills and waved them at Yingzhi. He yelled, "Take it all off and this money is yours!"

Yingzhi was bewildered. She seemed to see the image of Chunhui driving toward her from those bills. Then, all of a sud-den, Yingzhi reached back toward the strap of her dress. The audience immediately fell silent. Everyone was holding their breath as they stared at Yingzhi. Yingzhi continued to sing, but she turned her back to the audience. Then, one at a time, she undid her straps and let her dress slowly fall to the floor. Every-one saw Yingzhi standing there in her bra and G-string. Ying-zhi's G-string was extremely skimpy; it was so small that half her ass was already exposed. The hall broke out in a cacophony of cries and whistles. Yingzhi could hear Liu San's voice: "Yeah! What a body! That's hot! Take it all off!"

Yingzhi had never stood before an audience and experienced anything like this before. As she shook her hips and raised her arms she felt more carefree and light than ever before in her life. The roar of the crowd made her blood boil and set her body on fire. It was an almost unconscious action when she reached back to unhook her bra. It took only a gentle touch for her bra to fall to the floor. Her white breasts seemed a pair of birds extending their wings.

The old ancestral hall was in the throes of yet another climax as the audience roared. Liu San kept waving that money in front of Yingzhi. But the song ended. Yingzhi hadn't even taken everything off and it was already time for her to get off stage. Yingzhi took a curtain call and quickly picked up her clothes from the floor. She covered her breasts with her hands as she hurriedly hopped off the stage. Sanhuo grabbed a jacket, which he threw over Yingzhi's shoulders, and guided her into the warm changing room. He looked a bit disappointed as he said, "Yingzhi, you started stripping too late! If you had started a bit earlier, you could have taken everything off and that 500 yuan would have been yours!"

Yingzhi couldn't tell if she was cold or excited, but her whole body was shaking. She lost the ability to speak. Only after she sat down next to the heater and warmed herself for a few minutes did she finally heave a deep sigh of relief. Yingzhi realized that what Sanhuo said was right.

That day Yingzhi earned 302 yuan. Of that money, two hundred was from the tip that Liu San gave her. Xiaohong earned more than 500 yuan; as she counted her money, Xiaohong's eyes seemed to light up everything around her.

The men in the troupe earned very little. They didn't even bother looking at how much money they got; they just stuffed it into their pockets. One of them sighed and said he wished he had been born a girl. Wentang said, "If I had known you two were so willing to strip, I would have asked you to strip for us first! You know the saying 'Fertile water should be saved for your own field.' You should have kept the good stuff for us to enjoy! We could have scrambled together enough money to pay you!"

"Really?" Xiaohong immediately responded. "Do I have your word?"

But Yingzhi didn't say anything. She was still trying to figure out whether Wentang was being serious or just mocking them.

XI

The Lantern Festival had just passed. The cold wind had yet to blow away the shredded paper left behind from the dragon dance when the local county newspaper published an article by a university student who had returned home for the holidays. This university student had serious misgivings about the vulgar performances he had witnessed during Chinese New Year. The student asked whether society could ignore what might be unhealthy simply because it was fun. The article mentioned some theater troupes that featured inappropriate content, some variety shows that included superstitious elements, and some music groups that incorporated stripping into their act. After seeing these things, the author felt that the moral state of the village had rapidly deteriorated since he had left for college. This letter attracted the attention of provincial-level political leaders, who immediately launched an investigation and set out to rectify the situation.

It took only ten days' time for the Sanhuo Band's performance license to be revoked. The university student who published that letter had been from Wild Goose Village.

Just before the band officially disbanded, Sanhuo invited Yingzhi and a few other members of the troupe to lunch in town.

Sanhuo said that he initially thought that what happened in Wild Goose Village would make their business go through the roof; he never imagined that it would lead to the end of the Sanhuo Band. As he spoke, Sanhuo kept downing one drink after another, repeatedly sighing after each swig. Wentang kept toasting Sanhuo, and with each toast he cursed the university student who wrote that letter to the newspaper. He said that student was probably completely spoiled and after experiencing all the joys in life was fixed on making sure that other people couldn't enjoy their lives. By the third time Wentang cursed that student, Sanhuo interrupted him. "That student actually had a point," he said. "He's college educated and is a cultured person. Of course seeing something like that wouldn't sit well with him. Someone like him wants to see ballet dancers on their tippy toes, Western opera singers wearing those long gowns, and men wearing fancy tuxedos conducting big orchestras! Only that qualifies as being tasteful. Only that qualifies as true art! We just couldn't stand seeing how pathetic those villagers were and weren't quite sure how to liven things up, so we ended up coming up with this idea to make some money off them. It's only natural that it wouldn't sit right with some people."

"So in the future, what are the villagers supposed to do when they want to liven things up for weddings and funerals?" asked Yingzhi.

"Well, they won't be able to liven things up!" said Sanhuo. "When there are weddings, people will laugh; and when there are funerals, people will cry. But I guarantee you that just as many people will get married and just as many people will die!"

That made everyone at the table laugh. At the end of the meal, everyone said goodbye, but no one seemed particularly sad; they just said they'd try to start up again one day if the timing was right.

Yingzhi felt depressed the whole way home. She had originally hoped to speed up the timeline so that she could build her house more quickly. She never imagined that she would end up blowing up the whole thing. She thought about what Wentang said when he criticized that university student and completely agreed with everything he said.

Yingzhi didn't go directly home but instead followed Sanhuo and the others back to Phoenix Dike. It seemed that at her parents' house they were still celebrating Chinese New Year; a bunch of people were gathered around a table in the living room playing mah-jongg. They had a fire going, and it was quite toasty inside. Everyone started shouting when they saw Yingzhi come in. Yingzhi's sister-in-law immediately called her over to take her place at the mah-jongg table. Yingzhi waved her hand to refuse. Her mother was in the kitchen cooking; when she heard that Yingzhi had come home, she immediately rushed out of the kitchen, greeting her with a smile. She brought out all kinds of snacks like fried sesame paste leaves and peanuts. Being at her parents' house immediately felt so much more like home for Yingzhi.

Yingzhi took the snacks from her mother's hand; but instead of eating them, she pulled her mother's sleeve, leading her into one of the bedrooms. She said, "Mom, there's something I need to talk to you about."

Yingzhi's mother said, "I'm in the middle of cooking . . ."

"I'll be quick, then I have to get home," interrupted Yingzhi.

"You're not staying for dinner?" asked Yingzhi's mother.

"No, I really have to get home. Otherwise Guiqing will yell at me again," said Yingzhi.

"What's going on with the two of you?" asked Yingzhi's mother. "How could Guiqing be so heartless. I let my dear daughter marry him. Why doesn't he treat you better?"

Just hearing those words nearly brought Yingzhi to tears. She said, "It's all my in-laws' fault. They are always in the middle, causing trouble between us. Right now the only thing I want is to be able to move out and live apart from them."

"And how do you plan to do that?" asked Yingzhi's mother.

Yingzhi explained, "Guiqing and I plan to build another house. They have an empty plot of land next to their current house. Guiqing's parents already agreed to let us built it there. But as of now, we still don't have enough money. I was wondering . . . Mom, I was wondering if you might be willing to lend us a little?"

Yingzhi's mother said, "That's not something I can decide on my own. I'll have to talk it over with your father. I'll give you an answer later, okay?"

Yingzhi nodded. "Okay."

Yingzhi ended up staying at her parents' house for an extra day waiting for that answer. As soon as Yingzhi got out of bed the next morning, her mother pulled her into the kitchen and cooked her two poached eggs. There was a polite formality about the way she was waiting on her, as if Yingzhi wasn't her daughter. Yingzhi took one look at her mother's behavior and immediately knew that her father refused to let her borrow the money. Without waiting for her mother to explain, Yingzhi asked her directly, "Mom, Dad refused, didn't he?"

Yingzhi's mother awkwardly responded, "Yingzhi, your dad has his reasons. If your brothers learned that we wanted to lend you that money, there is no way they would ever agree. Especially since you are a girl."

Yingzhi grew angry. "And what's wrong with being a girl? Just because I'm your daughter, does that somehow mean that you and Dad didn't raise me?"

"I'm afraid that I have to go back to that old saying 'A daughter married off is like a basin of water that's been spilled on the ground.' As soon as you left this family, you became the property of another family. So of course there is a big difference between your situation and that of your brothers," explained Yingzhi's mother.

Yingzhi's anger intensified. "Over there, they never treat me like a part of their family. Over here, I'm nothing but a basin of spilled water. Everyone says both places are my home, but in reality neither of them is really my home! It is so unfair!"

"You're right, it is unfair," agreed Yingzhi's mother. "But for thousands of years this has been women's fate. What can we do? By the time you get to my age, you'll no longer think about it like that. You'll view your in-laws' family as your own—that's what happened with me."

Yingzhi didn't want to say anything else. She just ate her breakfast in silence, and then, without even saying goodbye, she slipped out the door alone. Hardly any people were out on the street. Whereas normally she could catch a ride home on a tractor, which would get her halfway to her house in twenty or thirty minutes, that morning Yingzhi ended up walking on and on without encountering any tractors. She barely encountered any other people as she passed through those open fields. Occasionally she would see someone working in the fields, and most of those people were old men. (It is hard to say exactly when everyone seemed to lose interest in doing farm work.)

Although the wind wasn't that strong, it was icy cold. Yingzhi forgot her scarf at her parents' house, and after walking for a while, she felt the cold wind sneaking down her collar. She raised her shoulders and tried to nestle her head close to her body to stay warm as she walked. The more she thought about what happened, the more choked up with resentment she became. *Everyone's been touting "gender equality" for so many years, so why the hell is it that no matter what happens, everything is always the woman's fault? Moreover, even women themselves somehow feel this is justified—take my mother, for instance. Just because your daughter gets married she's somehow no longer your own flesh and blood?* My in-laws' house has never been my true home, but now my parents also refuse to see me as part of their family—why are daughters faced with such a miserable fate? Only now did Yingzhi finally begin to understand why daughters all over the world cried when they married. She thought, *That's because the day a girl marries is the day she forever loses her sense of home. Here in this vast world, how many families have daughters that are left drifting? They are truly the saddest people in this world.*

Yingzhi carried those depressed thoughts with her as she arrived back at Old Temple Village. A few village loafers were hanging out sunning themselves near the foot of the wall at the village entrance; as soon as they saw Yingzhi, their eyes lit up. One of guys who went by the nickname Stink Bug shamelessly yelled out to her, "Yingzhi, how about we go down to the old temple so you can·strip for us?"

Yingzhi was shocked. She thought, *Shit, how did word travel so fast?* But she just laughed and said, "Strip!? I'll strip the skin right off your body, Stink Bug!"

Stink Bug snickered, "Yingzhi, everyone in the village is jealous of your husband! Everyone in Wild Goose Village is talking about you! They say your skin is whiter than snow on a cold winter's day!"

Yingzhi was getting close to blowing her fuse. "Fuck you! Stink Bug, you better watch out or I'll skin you alive!"

After cursing him, Yingzhi quickly moved on; she didn't dare linger a second longer than she needed to. She began to worry. Yingzhi knew that if these rumors made it to Guiqing's ears, she would be in for a rough time. Then Yingzhi remembered what Xiaohong had said about giving him 200 yuan and he wouldn't dare to lay a finger on her. Thinking about that,

Yingzhi decided to run by the local village convenience store to pick up a carton of cigarettes and two bottles of spirits for Guiqing; she also bought her in-laws two bottles of Sprite. As Yingzhi took the money out of her pocketbook to pay, she could feel her heart aching. The lady running the store flashed a strange smile as she said, "Ha, is this for Guiqing? Wow, the sun must have risen in the west this morning! Guiqing is one lucky man!"

Normally Yingzhi would have given her a piece of her mind right then and there, but that day she wasn't in the mood to pay attention to petty comments like that. All she was thinking about was how to deal with Guiqing when she got home.

From a distance Yingzhi could see the front gate of the house, which had just been painted with a new coat of black paint for the new year. It shone brightly. At that moment the front gate was tightly shut. That was unusual because whenever her in-laws were home, they usually kept the gate open. Yingzhi's heart began to pound. She tried to calm herself as she approached the gate. She called out in a gleeful tone, "Guiqing! Guiqing, come help me carry some of this in! Take a look at what I brought you!" As she pushed the gate open and went inside, she tried to act as naturally as possible.

Yingzhi's in-laws both had long faces as they sat upright at the table in the living room. Those words *Heaven, Earth, Ruler, Parents, Teacher* were still hanging above them. Yingzhi put the bottles of Sprite down on the table and smiled. "I bought these two bottles of soda for you."

Yingzhi's father-in-law let out a disdainful grumble while her mother-in-law extended her sharp fingers and pointed straight at Yingzhi's nose, yelling in a shrill voice, "You piece of trash! You bought this with the money you made selling your dirty cunt! You're going to drive us to our graves!"

The sharp, shrill sound of her mother-in-law's voice made Yingzhi feel as if a needle were being driven into her ear, piercing her eardrum. Yingzhi never imagined that her mother-in-law would start things off like that. She immediately defended herself: "What's wrong? I didn't do anything that would be considered shameful."

That's when Guiqing rushed in from his bedroom and grabbed hold of Yingzhi's hair. Yingzhi immediately started to scream. Guiqing shouted at her, "You filthy bitch! I gave you permission to go out and earn extra money singing. I never told you to take off your clothes! Do you have no shame? You're so desperate for money that you've gone crazy! Is money more important than your dignity? When it comes to being a whore, you're a fucking natural! I must have been blind to have married you!"

Guiqing kept slapping her as he yelled. Yingzhi could feel her face already swelling. She instinctively resisted, kicking Guiqing as her arms thrashed around. She cried out, "And what if I do want to make money? What's wrong with that? If you're able to, why don't you go out and make some money to support your wife!?"

"You fucking bitch! Even now you dare to speak back to me!" Guiqing yelled.

Yingzhi kicked Guiqing in the balls. He groaned in pain and released his grip as he reached down to hold his groin.

Yingzhi took the opportunity to run for the door. She thought, *My God, there is no way I'm going to let him beat me to death*. She made it out to the courtyard only to discover that her father-in-law had already beaten her there. He locked the front gate, and she didn't know where the key was. Her father-in-law flashed her a cold smile before returning to the house. Guiqing came outside holding a stick. He roared at her, "You fucking bitch, you kicked me in the balls and you think I'm going to let you live after that!" Guiqing raised the stick to hit her. Yingzhi tried to dodge the blow, which missed her face but came down on her shoulder.

Yingzhi screamed in pain and fell to the ground. She couldn't stand up, but she started crawling toward the pigpen. Guiqing followed behind her, wildly swinging the stick at her as she pulled herself along the ground.

Eventually she found herself backed up against the pigpen. There was nowhere else for her to go. Consumed by a mixture of grief and indignation, Yingzhi thought, *Go ahead and hit me. What's the worst you can do? Kill me? I'd rather be dead than go on living like this.* As those thoughts cycled through her head, she unconsciously continued to struggle; she curled herself into a ball against the wall of the pigpen as Guiqing continued to beat her. He hit her so much that Yingzhi could no longer feel the pain and passed out.

By the time she woke up, it was already sometime in the afternoon. One of the pigs was lying beside her, and its foul smell assaulted her nose. She managed to crawl away but didn't dare enter the house; she instead headed for the main gate. By this time the gate was open. Yingzhi made it through the gate and was struck by how bright it was outside.

Yingzhi staggered her way out of Old Temple Village. Her cotton jacket had been ripped open by Guiqing and several pieces of cotton were sticking out. Dried-up blood from her battered, swollen face had dribbled all the way down to her neck. Her mind remained blank; all she knew was that she had to keep going forward. She didn't even know if she was heading in the right direction to get home. So it was a good thing that the road home was a path she didn't have to think about; it was engraved in her mind.

It was nearly dusk by the time she finally arrived at her parents' house. Her nephew, Shaoya, was the first one to notice that she was home. Shaoya immediately started to scream, "Grandpa! Grandma! . . . Look what happened to Auntie!"

Everyone in the house rushed outside to see. Yingzhi could hear a cacophony of footsteps approaching her, but before she could see anyone's face, she collapsed onto the ground.

XII

Yingzhi rested at her parents' house for an entire week. She never even got out of bed. When Yingzhi's parents and brothers saw her entire body covered with bruises, they were so angry that they started rubbing their fists—they wanted to kill Guiqing. Yingzhi's father and two brothers gathered up around a dozen able-bodied young men from Phoenix Dike and set out for Old Temple Village. Yingzhi's oldest brother said that all blood debts must be paid in kind; they would never let that bastard Guiqing get away with what he had done. But as soon as Guiqing explained his reason for beating his wife, Yingzhi's father and brothers were utterly shocked. In the end, they not only did not lay a finger on Guiqing but also repeatedly apologized to him. The whole way home they were all completely dejected.

But Yingzhi didn't know about any of this.

The day Yingzhi finally got out of bed was bright and sunny. The wounds on Yingzhi's body had begun to scab over, but the wound in her heart continued bleeding. After breakfast Yingzhi stood by the window gazing up at the sun outside. Her nephew, Shaoya, and her niece, Chrysanthemum, were outside laughing and chasing each other under the sun. Yingzhi wondered what her little Jianhuo was doing at that moment.

Yingzhi's father came in and silently sat down with a frustrated look on his face. Yingzhi looked at him but had no idea why he was so upset. After clearing his throat a few times, he finally spoke: "When you're wrong, you need to fess up and admit it. Go home and apologize to Guiqing, and give him a gift to show him you're sincere. You can't stay here for the rest of your life. A woman like you should know that there are rules when it comes to what types of behavior are allowed and what types are unacceptable."

Yingzhi could feel her head spinning. She understood what her father meant. And yet here she was having been beaten to a pulp, scars and bruises all over her body, and not only did no one apologize to her but also now her father wanted *her* to go and beg for forgiveness! She felt as if those half-healed wounds on her body would suddenly burst open, as if she were being ripped apart. She wanted to howl like an animal, she wanted to bash her head against the wall, she wanted to rip her chest open, she wanted to scream to the gods, *Why do you treat women so unfairly?*

Seeing how the expression on his daughter's face changed, Yingzhi's father reached into his pocket and took out a pile of bills. "This is 3,000 yuan; it's all the money we have, but I'm going to lend it to you for now. You and Guiqing build your house and live a good life together. Don't do anything else that will make us all lose face again."

Yingzhi's father put the money down on the table and walked away. As he retreated, his footsteps had a heavy, frustrated cadence. The sunlight shone through the window and onto the table, where that pile of cash seemed to glow under the sunlight, its rays reflecting out in all directions. The glow seemed to melt away Yingzhi's anger. She gradually approached the table and picked up that pile of bills; finding some paper, she carefully wrapped up the money and tucked it into her pocket. Yingzhi took no other objects when she left. She just went into the kitchen to say goodbye to her mother. "Mom, I'm going now!"

Yingzhi's mother was adding firewood to keep the stove going and turned around to say, "My child, you need to face your fate. You're a woman, and you need to remember that a woman's fate is to take good care of her man. Don't fight with him; you'll never win."

Yingzhi hit the road alone. She felt as if she were in a trance as she walked. In that trancelike state she wondered, *When did I ever fight with him?* It was afternoon by the time Yingzhi saw the houses of Old Temple Village in the midst of that forest of green trees. Her heart started racing, unsure of what was awaiting her this time. A few people were hanging out at the village entrance, and when they saw Yingzhi coming, they rushed off to report to Guiqing.

It wasn't long after Yingzhi entered the village that she saw Guiqing. He was standing there big and tall under the winter sun. Yingzhi immediately felt her legs grow weak. She was struck by such fear that she didn't dare take another step forward. Guiqing approached her. "You're back? I was just getting ready to head down to your village to fetch you."

Yingzhi lowered her head but didn't say anything. Guiqing said, "Did you know, earlier today Jianhuo was running around the village chasing after a dog and he fell down. As soon as he fell he called out for his mom. It was a shame you weren't here to see it. He is really something."

Yingzhi was about to break down in tears, but still she didn't say a word. They went into the house together, and Yingzhi immediately started looking for Jianhuo. As she picked her son up, all the day's accumulated tears poured out. Afraid that Guiqing might see her cry, she buried her face in Jianhuo's clothes.

But Guiqing noticed nonetheless and said, "You just got home. What's there to cry about?"

"I missed Jianhuo so much," replied Yingzhi.

That night Guiqing tried to help Yingzhi out of her clothes, but Yingzhi pulled away. Guiqing said, "Don't tell me that I can't even help you get undressed?"

"You think I'm willing to let anyone see my body right now?" said Yingzhi.

"I don't care," said Guiqing. "You're my wife and I want to see!" Guiqing forcefully removed Yingzhi's clothing, exposing the bruises and wounds all over her body. The sight shocked Guiqing. Yingzhi faced the wall and began to cry again. In that moment Guiqing was filled with remorse; he caressed the wounds on her body. "Yingzhi, I don't know what I was thinking," he said. "I had no idea that I hit you so hard. I must have gone really mad. Don't cry, Yingzhi. Get up and hit me back. Use the stick. C'mon, I deserve it." As Guiqing spoke, he got out of bed to look for the stick.

"What's the point of hitting you? Could I ever really win against you?" said Yingzhi.

Guiqing kneeled down and said, "Yingzhi, I'm sorry. If you can somehow see in your heart not to hate me, I promise that from this day forward I'll do whatever you ask me to do. But please don't hate me. You know that I actually really love you."

Yingzhi thought about what he said for a moment and replied, "If you really love me, show me with your actions. All I want is for us to build a house of our own, I don't care about the rest."

"Done. We'll build it! That's what I was planning on telling you. My parents have already agreed. The only problem is the money . . ." began Guiqing.

That's when Yingzhi said, "My parents lent me some money. I also have some savings from the money I earned. Let's just start building with the money we have now. We'll see how far we can get with the construction."

"No problem! Whatever you want. We can start tomorrow."

That night Guiqing had another long tryst with Yingzhi; they ended up carrying on until the middle of the night before Guiqing finally fell asleep. But Yingzhi was so excited by her husband's promise that she couldn't get to sleep.

Yingzhi and Guiqing finally began to build their house. Guiqing had done work in renovations, so he knew some of the basics when it came to building a house. He started off by sketching a rough blueprint based on Yingzhi's specifications. It was to be a two-story house facing south. In the middle of the first floor would be a large living room, with two rooms on either side. The rooms facing south would be Jianhuo's bedroom and another bedroom for a second son; the rooms facing north would be a storage room for tools and miscellaneous items and a guest room. The kitchen would be next to the storage room. There would be an outside staircase to get up to the second floor, with a pig shed built in beneath the stairs. Yingzhi and Guiqing's master bedroom would be upstairs. Since Yingzhi had talked about it so many times, Guiqing also added an indoor toilet to the blueprint—that was the detail that made Yingzhi most happy. Guiqing was also planning to install a shower in the bathroom, which would make washing much more convenient. That was a detail that Yingzhi hadn't even thought of, and she made sure to compliment her husband for thinking of it. There were two more rooms upstairs. Guiqing explained, "In case we have a girl, it will be better to let her stay upstairs close to us." Yingzhi thought, *I don't want a girl. If I bring a girl into this world to suffer and be humiliated, I'm not sure I could take that as a mother.* But since she was in such a good mood, she decided to keep those thoughts to herself.

Yingzhi and Guiqing started going out to buy supplies like bricks and cement. Yingzhi even went back to her parents' house to borrow her brother's walking tractor for a few days; Guiqing drove that tractor around picking up all the materials. After spending nearly a month purchasing all the supplies, they were finally ready to start construction. They broke ground on the new house on March 8, a date that Yingzhi had chosen. Guiqing asked, "Is March 8, Women's Day, considered an auspicious date?"

"That's the date I want!" insisted Yingzhi. She was thinking that since it was Women's Day, perhaps she could finally use this date to turn things around for herself.

They used Yingzhi's money to purchase all the building materials; Guiqing hadn't contributed a cent of his own money. Even those days when they were out in town to pick up materials and had to buy a steamed bun or a bowl of noodles, it was always Yingzhi who footed the bill. This put Guiqing in a somewhat awkward position and didn't leave him much leeway when it came to negotiating various details with Yingzhi.

On March 8 the peach blossoms behind Yingzhi's house suddenly bloomed. In years past they had never bloomed so early, so Yingzhi couldn't help taking it as an auspicious sign. As they got to work, everyone looked at those peach blossoms; someone asked Yingzhi what she was so happy about. Perhaps the flowers meant that Guiqing was up for some peach-blossom romance! Yingzhi laughed, "Once his peach-blossom luck gets going, I don't think anyone will be able to stop him! Let his peach-blossom luck roll; meanwhile I'll stick with my dogshit luck!"

It was rare to see Yingzhi so happy and make jokes like that. Everyone broke out in a wave of laughter. Guiqing was also in a good mood, and he really put his back into his work. But every night after a long day's work, Guiqing would invite his buddies who were helping with the construction out to eat at a roadside restaurant; over dinner they would start drinking, and after that they would start to play mah-jongg. Yingzhi was the one who ended up having to cover all those extra expenses. She didn't mind spending her money on the house, but seeing them eat away her money each night on food and entertainment was tearing her apart. There were several times that she put on a long face and told Guiqing that it was fine to take his buddies out a few times, but not every single day! But Guiqing gave what he thought was a perfectly justified response: "You can't ask them to break their backs working every day and not feed them every day!"

Yingzhi had no good answer to that.

The house went up quickly. It took only a few days' time for all the prefabricated slab walls to go up. A few days later the roof went up and the house started to really take shape. All the prepurchased construction materials had been used, but much work remained to be done. Besides putting in the flooring and doing the painting, they still needed to install all the windows and doors, and the bathroom Yingzhi had been waiting for was completely empty. There were also many things that still needed to be purchased. Guiqing wrote up a list detailing how much lime, sand, cement, and paint was needed. Yingzhi went through the list carefully checking the prices and amounts with Guiqing. She stayed up all night calculating, but no matter how much they penny-pinched, they were going to be at least 3,000 yuan short—and that didn't include the cost of a main gate and court-yard wall. Yingzhi had less than 1,000 yuan left; there was no way she was going to have enough money to finish construction. She sat up the entire night fretting over what to do.

Guiqing arrived home yawning after a late game of mah-jongg. Yingzhi told him they were going to be short and asked him what they should do. She was implying that Guiqing should ask his parents for a loan, but Guiqing pretended not to hear. Seeing his attitude, Yingzhi was on the verge of losing it with him. But rather than confront him, she decided to bring the matter up directly with her in-laws.

That morning Yingzhi didn't rush out to the construction site to check on the new house as usual; instead, she went into the kitchen to help her mother-in-law make porridge. She squatted next to the oven putting firewood into the stove to feed the fire; Yingzhi reminded herself that she needed to be patient. Yingzhi's mother-in-law flashed her a cold smile, then said, "It's been nearly two years since you married into our family. I don't think you've stepped into the kitchen once! For some reason I have a hard time believing you are really here to help me make porridge."

Her mother-in-law's words left Yingzhi momentarily speechless. She hemmed and hawed before finally saying, "Here's the deal . . . Mom, our house . . . well, you've seen it; it's almost finished. But . . . but . . . we spent all our money and we need a little bit more to . . ."

Yingzhi hadn't finished when her mother-in-law interrupted. "Your father-in-law and I actually do have a bit of money saved up, but don't you ever dream that I would one day lend any of it to you to build your house! That money is for our retirement. Seeing the dissolute lifestyle you lead, I know I'll never be able to count on you and Guiqing to take care of us. So you can show up here in the kitchen and help me get the stove going for a hundred days and you're still not getting one penny from me . . ."

Yingzhi didn't wait for her mother-in-law to finish her sentence either. She angrily shoved the last piece of firewood in her hand into the oven, stood up, and walked out. As she left the room, Yingzhi thought, *Just listening to those despicable words makes it clear to me that no one would ever be able to tolerate her!*

Construction on the new house came to a halt. According to Guiqing, they had already made great progress. From here on out, they would just have to finish the rest step by step as money came in. As long as they kept chipping away at it, the house would eventually be finished. Yingzhi thought that made sense. But being forced to continue living under the same roof as her in-laws—eating together, going in and out through the same door—was driving her crazy. For her, family wasn't a warm happy place—it was her own personal hell. The more she thought about it, the more convinced Yingzhi became that she had to find a way to quickly finish the house and get away from her in-laws.

That day after lunch Yingzhi told Guiqing that she was going home to try to borrow some more money from her parents. Guiqing agreed and, as he was seeing her out the door, he sarcastically muttered, "I don't get why you asked my parents for money when you've got all that cash at your parents' house just sitting there! You're just asking for trouble!"

The color immediately drained from Yingzhi's face as she silently cursed him: *You think my family runs a bank? Moreover, I'm building a house in your village and when it's done, you are the one who's going to live in it! Why should I have to borrow money from my parents? Your parents are worthless. There is no point even cursing them! People like Guiqing think only about what's in their own best interest; yelling at them is of no use. If I want to hate some-one, I can only hate myself for marrying the wrong man . . . and now I'm stuck with no way out.* As Yingzhi walked home, she became increasingly convinced that marriage for a woman is either heaven or hell. If you marry the right person, it is heaven; but if you marry the wrong person, it is hell. Sanhuo's wife mar-ried into heaven; she herself married into hell. Yingzhi hated herself for not realizing this when she was still a young girl.

She absentmindedly jumped into marriage with Guiqing. And as if marrying an irresponsible playboy like Guiqing wasn't bad enough, she also got stuck with the worst in-laws imaginable. She wondered if she had done something terrible in her previous life to justify such punishment.

As she walked along and thought about her predicament, she ended up heading straight toward the county seat. She decided to visit Wentang to see if he would lend her some money.

Wentang was in charge of the sound at a disco called Tap Dance. As soon as he laid eyes on Yingzhi, Wentang flashed her a sly smile and crooned, "Did you miss me?"

Wentang never took anything seriously, and standing before him immediately set Yingzhi at ease. She laughed. "What's there worth missing? The only thing I miss is the money in your wallet!"

"Of course I knew that! When I asked if you missed me, what I meant was, Did you miss my money? I wouldn't dare think that you actually missed me as a person!" Wentang joked.

"You're a fucking scoundrel! You really know how to drag someone down with your sarcasm!" said Yingzhi.

"Aren't you supposed to be busy building your new house? Since when do you have time to come into town?" asked Wentang.

"That's what I'm here for. I have to be honest with you, Wentang. I actually did come here to borrow some money from you. The house is almost done, but I need another 3,000 yuan to finish it. Can you spot me the cash? I promise to pay you back next year," said Yingzhi.

Wentang flashed her a sidelong glance and smiled. "I'm happy to lend you the money . . . but what's in it for me?"

"I promise to pay you back every cent, including whatever the going interest rate is at the bank," said Yingzhi.

"The interest rate offered by the bank is practically nothing," said Wentang.

"Then . . . what else do you want?" asked Yingzhi.

Wentang pulled Yingzhi close to him. "Don't tell me you don't know what I want? We've always had a close relationship, but whenever we were together, you gave me only a little taste . . . you know I want more."

"You're really quite the ambitious one, now, aren't you? You're not afraid that your wife might castrate you?" joked Yingzhi.

"I'll just be sure she doesn't find out. Let me tell you, Yingzhi, at one point Xiaohong wanted to sleep with me, but I didn't do it. That dirty bitch sleeps with everybody. Heaven knows what kind of crazy STDs you'll pick up if you fuck her! That shit could kill you! But you're different. You talk dirty, but when it comes down to it, you haven't slept with anyone besides Guiqing, isn't that so?"

"I guess you really do understand something about me," Yingzhi said.

"We only live once. We should try to be happy while we're here, no?" Wentang said. "You see how Guiqing treats you. You're foolish to remain faithful to him. Wouldn't it be great to have a lover besides Guiqing? You'll feel much happier and be in a better mood. What's more, your lover can also supply you with some money. Hell, he can even lend you the money for your new house!"

Yingzhi had been listening closely, up until that last sentence. She couldn't avoid bursting out laughing, "You act like you 're lecturing me on the meaning of life, and then, all of a sudden, you make it all about yourself! Men are fucking bastards!"

"Why should you care if a man is a bastard or not? As long as you get your loan, isn't that enough?" said Wentang.

Yingzhi thought about it and realized there was some sense to what Wentang said. She always had a decent impression of

Wentang; moreover, whenever they fooled around in the past, he always paid her for it. As a woman, all she ever really wanted in life was love. But before that love could even be born, it was extinguished. Perhaps she also wanted the warmth of a family, but the family she was now stuck with was a living hell. Since she couldn't have any of the things she really wanted, why couldn't she at least have money? Why couldn't she have a little fun for herself with this man who was now throwing himself at her?

All these thoughts flashed through Yingzhi's mind like lightning. Wentang seemed to already have her figured out. He leaned in to whisper in her ear, "The private room over there is empty; no one will ever know."

Thinking that she might actually hook up with Wentang made Yingzhi feel a touch of shame. Wentang laughed heartily. "My dear Yingzhi, I never imagined that you were such a fair maiden!"

In Yingzhi's mind, being compared with a "fair maiden" was so ridiculous that it made her crack up laughing. That laughter loosened her up, and she said, "Fuck your little fair maiden!"

XIII

By the time Yingzhi left Wentang's Tap Dance club, it was already four o'clock in the afternoon. After being with Wentang, Yingzhi realized just how different the experience of sleeping with another man could be. Wentang wanted Yingzhi to stay for dinner before leaving. He said that she made him feel things other women never did and he wanted to thank her. Yingzhi refused. It wasn't that she didn't want to eat dinner; she was afraid that going back late carrying so much money might not be a good idea. Wentang agreed and didn't insist, but he was extremely loving as he saw her off at the bus station. As they said goodbye, Yingzhi gave him a playful slap on the cheek. "Stop pretending to be romantic!"

Wentang laughed. "Who says I'm a romantic? I'm just sad to see that money in your pocket leave me!"

Yingzhi was in a wonderful mood the whole way home. She put the money in the pocket of her long underwear. Long underwear usually doesn't have pockets, but in order to hide her money, Yingzhi had sewn a pocket in the belly area. The pocket was stitched closed on all four sides, with the exception of a small one-inch slit on top. Whenever she put money in, she had to fold it up so that it would fit through the slit and then used her finger to slowly even it out from the outside. This was a little trick she learned back when she was with the Sanhuo Band. It was only when she could physically feel the money pressing up against her belly that she had a real sense of security. For some reason the 3,000 yuan she got this time felt like more money than last time; it took forever to squeeze all those bills into her secret pocket. Even with Wentang helping her, she still couldn't get all the bills completely flat. It was a good thing that it was still cold out and people were still wearing several layers of clothes; except for her stomach protruding a little, there was nothing about her appearance that really stood out. Wentang couldn't help cracking a joke: "I slept with you only once and already your stomach is getting big!" Yingzhi couldn't stop laughing in response. She thought, *Maybe my son really isn't more important than money. If you have money but no son, you can still live a great life. Money will help you through all the various challenges in life. But if you have a son but no money, you're done for. If something bad should happen, will you really be able to count on your son to help you?* Thinking about it like that, Yingzhi felt a warmth coming from that wad of money pressed up against her belly, a warmth that went straight to her heart. When she left home that afternoon, she was in a terrible mood, but any trace of that was now gone: it was as if the sun had risen from her stomach and its rays of light had melted that sour mood away.

When Yingzhi returned home, Guiqing was still out playing mah-jongg. Her in-laws had already had dinner, so Yingzhi went into the kitchen to find something to eat, but not a scrap of food was left. Yingzhi could barely contain her frustration, so she impatiently asked her mother-in-law, "How come you didn't leave me even a bowl of rice?"

Yingzhi's mother-in-law answered, "Didn't you say you were going back to your parents' house? I thought they had a big bundle of money to give you. Don't tell me they can't afford to give you a bowl of rice?"

That response left Yingzhi speechless. It took Yingzhi a few minutes before she said, "I didn't want to come home too late, so I left before dinner. I never said that I'd be having dinner at my parents' house."

But Yingzhi's mother-in-law commented, "I wouldn't dare cook extra rice if I didn't think we needed it. If you and Guiqing don't come home to eat, what am I supposed to do with all that leftover food? Feed it to the pigs? We're a poor family. I don't dare to waste food."

Yingzhi filled up a bowl with water from the vat they used for drinking water. As she slurped down the water, the ill will of her mother-in-law's words hit her like a ton of bricks, completely shattering the good mood she had been in just ten minutes earlier. The surge of ill will also ignited Yingzhi's own hostility: she took the bowl in her hand and smashed it on the floor, scattering shards of shattered porcelain and splashing water everywhere. Yingzhi howled, "If there's no rice, there's no rice! But why the hell do you need to speak to me like that?"

Yingzhi's sudden action so shocked her mother-in-law that she took a few steps back; as she backed up, she tripped on a wooden stool and ended up falling to the floor. Yingzhi's father-in-law heard the commotion and rushed over. He saw his wife sitting on the floor surrounded by broken pieces of porcelain and small puddles of water, and there was his daughter-in-law standing over her screaming in anger. Yingzhi's father-in-law immediately lost his temper. He slapped Yingzhi across the face and yelled, "You're evil! You dare raise your hand to your mother-in-law! Don't you have even the most basic sense of dignity?"

Yingzhi knew that once her father-in-law lost his temper, she was bound to end up on the losing side; so rather than answer back, she buried her face in her hands and ran back into her bedroom. Why was everything so difficult for her? Yingzhi had so much pent-up anger that she started to feel chest pains. No matter how much she cried, screamed, or cursed, nothing was able to relieve the anger and resentment that consumed her. The only thing left for her to do was to pound the headboard of her bed; she kept hitting it until her entire hand became enflamed.

Guiqing stayed at the mah-jongg table all night and didn't drag himself home until almost sunrise. He didn't say a word when he came in but just collapsed on the bed; it took only a few seconds before he started snoring. Yingzhi nudged Guiqing a few times with her elbow, but he just grumbled some foul words and continued snoring.

Yingzhi couldn't get back to sleep; she just lay there in bed with her eyes open until dawn.

Yingzhi finished her breakfast, but seeing that Guiqing still hadn't risen, she took Jianhuo out to play in the village. A group of old ladies were sitting under the Chinese scholar tree near the village ancestral hall weaving slippers. When they saw Yingzhi, they called her over and asked her to sit down with them. They told her that they had never seen a woman as strong as Yingzhi before; it was amazing that she had gone out and earned all the money to build a new house. All the men in Old Temple Village were useless, they said, and their wives had no choice but to share their fate and go on living in old dilapidated houses. Yingzhi was the only one who was different: her man may have been useless, but she was a capable woman. They said that what she did really showed everyone that women were able to fight for a better life. Yingzhi was all smiles when she heard that; she finally thought that at least someone in this world understood her.

As the sun rose higher in the sky, she caught sight of her father-in-law heading out to the forest carrying his pesticide equipment. Suspecting that Guiqing must be up by now, she picked up Jianhuo to go home. Having already eaten breakfast, Guiqing had his legs up in a carefree pose as if there was nothing for him to do. As Yingzhi came in, she put Jianhuo down and smirked at Guiqing. "Finally up? You slept an hour longer than the pigs outside!"

Guiqing lazily replied, "I don't have anything better to do. What's wrong with sleeping in?"

"Well, now I've got something for you to do," said Yingzhi. "I was able to borrow some money yesterday. Why don't you go out today to purchase the rest of the supplies we need to finish the house?"

Guiqing's eyes instantly lit up and a smile appeared on his face. Yingzhi looked at him with a perplexed stare; something was off about him. She said, "Just buy the things on the list from last time. I wrote down all the prices, so don't spend any more than what's indicated."

"Don't worry, I'm an expert haggler!" boasted Guiqing.

"Make sure you go now and come back by the afternoon. We can then ask your buddies to come tomorrow morning to start work again. The quicker we get this done, the better," asserted Yingzhi.

"Great plan! I can't wait to get started!" exclaimed Guiqing.

Yingzhi licked her fingers as she counted the money, handing all the bills over to Guiqing. She said, "All together that's 3,000 yuan. Make sure you get receipts for all the purchases so that I can check the numbers later. There are still a few things we need to buy for the new house with any money that's left over."

"That's right, we need to make the new house nice and comfortable. We'll live like city people! But the air here is much better than in the city!"

As Yingzhi handed the money over to Guiqing, she kept reminding him to tuck it away properly. Guiqing pounded his chest and looked Yingzhi in the eye as he hastily said, "You can rest assured. I promise we'll be completely settled into the new house within two months!"

The way Guiqing took the money from Yingzhi's hands was almost as if he were stealing it. The second he got his hands on the cash, he shoved it into the pocket of his undershirt and ran straight out the door. For a moment Yingzhi was struck with an ominous feeling. She didn't understand why he was acting like that. She followed him out the door, and as Guiqing retreated into the distance, she called out, "Come back soon!"

A strange happiness filled Yingzhi as she waited at home. By late afternoon Guiqing had not yet returned, but Yingzhi knew that it was a tall order to go all the way out to the county seat to purchase all those materials in just a few hours. That afternoon Yingzhi kept going outside to look at the construction site. From the second-story balcony of the new house you could see all the way out to the village entrance. She kept going up there hoping she could see Guiqing as soon as he returned.

She must have gone up there five times throughout the day. But all was quiet out by the village entrance; there were no signs of people. So she just walked around the construction site, looking over all the details of her new house. She was quite familiar with what parts needed to be completed and which areas were awaiting supplies; she also had carefully planned out what pictures she was going to hang up and how to decorate the place. Even though the railing on the second-floor balcony hadn't been put up yet, being up there gave Yingzhi a wonderful feeling. She could look down and see her in-laws walking in and out of their house below. They were so old, both of them were stooped over, and she could intermittently hear the sound of their coughing. They wouldn't last more than a few more years, and when that time came, Yingzhi would be the mistress of these two houses.

Just thinking about that excited Yingzhi. It should take only another month or so to finish the house, and she decided that once she moved in, she would sit up there every day to watch the people in the distance and listen to the sounds as they gradually grew fainter. She cherished the thought of what an amazing life that would be.

The sun gradually set over Yingzhi's happy thoughts. As dusk came, all the oxen and sheep slowly returned to their pens. A few children were returning from the fields riding on an ox's back; the sound of their giggles and cries gradually made their way to Yingzhi's ears. Another person flew past on a bicycle. The view of the village entrance became hazy as the sky darkened. Finally, some people in the village began to turn on their lights; those lights were faint but bright enough to penetrate the darkness and make their way to Yingzhi's eyes. But Guiqing hadn't yet returned home.

Yingzhi began to grow anxious but didn't know what she should do. She had no appetite and skipped dinner to go over to Youjie's house to see if he knew where Guiqing was. Youjie wasn't home, so she went to Fatty's house; he wasn't home either. Yingzhi was so upset that she stamped her feet and cursed, "Where the hell did those fucking guys go?"

It was midnight when Guiqing finally returned. Yingzhi was lying in bed exhausted; she figured that Guiqing must have run into some kind of trouble to return so late. As soon as she heard his voice calling to open the gate, she excitedly leaped out of bed. Without even bothering to find her slippers, she ran out to the courtyard barefooted to greet him. As soon as she opened the gate, she launched into a series of questions: "Why are you home so late? Where are the construction materials? Did you get everything? Were there any problems? Nobody ripped you off, did they? How much money is left?"

Guiqing didn't even have a chance to respond. He just stood there outside the gate. Once Yingzhi finish her round of questions, he dejectedly muttered, "Let's go inside to talk."

Seeing the state he was in, Yingzhi's heart grew cold. She quickly asked, "What happened? Did you get the stuff?"

Guiqing lowered his head and walked toward the bedroom, ignoring her questions. Yingzhi was so anxious that she felt as if she could barely breathe. She grabbed hold of Guiqing's arm. "I need you to explain what exactly happened."

"You really want me to tell you now?" asked Guiqing.

"Yes, let's have it!" demanded Yingzhi.

"I didn't buy anything," confessed Guiqing.

"Why not?" asked Yingzhi.

"Just as I was leaving the village, I ran into Youjie and the rest of the guys. They invited me to hang out. I thought I'd still have time to make it to the county seat by the afternoon. So we went over to General Village, but once we got into the game, I completely forgot to buy the stuff."

Furious, Yingzhi scolded, "All you know how to do is have fun! I asked you to do a simple task and you couldn't even do that! Where's the money? Give it to me and I'll give it back to you tomorrow when it is time to go back to buy the stuff."

"I'll give it back to you in a few days," said Guiqing.

Yingzhi's heart tightened as an ominous feeling assaulted her. Her voice trembled as she asked, "Why? What happened?"

Guiqing was getting annoyed by all her questions; he just waved her away with his hand and went into the bedroom. As he walked away he said, "Don't ask, okay? If I tell you, you'll only get more upset."

Yingzhi yelled, "You better believe that I'm going to ask you! It's my money. I need to know what happened!"

Guiqing responded, "Three words: I lost it."

Yingzhi stopped in a state of shock. This was much, much worse than anything she could have imagined.

Guiqing, on the other hand, acted as if it was no big deal. He said, "I told you not to ask. I knew you'd get upset."

Yingzhi felt as if all the blood in her body were going to explode through every pore. She felt as if something were tearing her internal organs apart. She thought she was losing her mind. She was about to scream but held it in and instead pounced on Guiqing like a rabid dog, clawing at his face, immediately leaving behind several red marks across his cheeks. Guiqing reached up to protect his face, but he didn't hit back. Yingzhi's scratches quickly turned into punches, then she picked up a broom and tried hitting Guiqing in the face with it as she hysterically screamed, "Give it back! Give me back my money!" Her voice was tinged with a shrill, almost crazed tone. Guiqing just stood there staring at her, not knowing what to do. It never occurred to him to hit her back.

When Yingzhi's in-laws heard the ruckus, they quickly threw on their clothes and rushed over to see what was happening. The first thing they saw was Yingzhi hitting their son.

As soon as Yingzhi's mother-in-law saw the red marks on her son's face, she started screaming, "Heavens, you're trying to kill my son! Guiqing, my dear son, why don't you beat this evil witch to death?"

Standing there holding his cheek, Guiqing heard his mother's screams and snapped out of his daze. It was as if Yingzhi's crazed appearance forced him to momentarily confront his own guilt. He didn't dare look Yingzhi in the eye and instead barked at his mother, "It's none of your business! I want her to hit me!"

Guiqing's father slammed his hand down on the table and yelled, "You fucking bastard! And you call yourself a man? How can you let your wife hit you like that? She deserves to be beaten to death! If you don't kill that bitch, how are you supposed to ever have any dignity?"

Guiqing turned to yell at his father. "She's my wife, why the hell should I beat her to death? What if I like it when she hits me? You got a problem with that?"

Yingzhi's in-laws were completely dumbfounded by their son's words. They looked at each other for a moment before sighing and returning to their room, all the while cursing under their breath.

Yingzhi just stood there frozen as Guiqing cursed at his parents. She had never heard him yell at them like that. Her head felt as if it would explode, but she didn't know why. She didn't know what to do and just stood there frozen for a while before walking off. She was facing the front gate, and so that is the direction she went, walking right out through that gate.

Guiqing called out after her, but she didn't respond. Yingzhi just kept walking forward; she walked on and on until her feet started to ache, and only then did she snap out of her daze and realize that she wasn't even wearing shoes. She wondered why she didn't have shoes on. Then she started to piece together everything that had just happened. She broke down in tears. She kept crying as she walked, leaving a trail of tears behind her.

The only place Yingzhi could go was to her parents' house. But what could they do to help her? All they could do was use some simple words of encouragement to try to cheer her up while they cursed Guiqing. Once she felt better, they just told her to try to bear it for the sake of Jianhuo. And in the end they just told her that this was all a matter of fate.

But Yingzhi couldn't get past what had happened and screamed, "Why does this have to be my fate? How come no matter what I do, I can't change my fate? I want to get a divorce!"

Yingzhi's father jumped to his feet to yell, "All you do is fight and argue. All your drama has made everyone in this family lose face! And now you want a fucking divorce! If you dare to try divorcing him, I'll break your legs!"

Yingzhi's father's words came down like a final judgment. After that no one dared to say anything else. Yingzhi's mother's heart ached for her daughter, but she didn't know how she could help her. All she could do was console her. "Yingzhi, my baby. You've had a tough fate. It's been tougher for you than for most people. But no matter how hard it is, you need to learn to accept things. What else can you do? If you were to really get a divorce, all that hard work that went into saving up to build that house of yours would be wasted. And it would crush Guiqing and his family. My child, divorce simply isn't worth it."

What her mother said really had a powerful impact on Yingzhi. She realized her mother was right, she couldn't get a divorce; if she divorced, all her hard work these past few years would be wasted. Her house, her dreams, all would go up in smoke. Perhaps Guiqing would remarry and he and his new wife would move into the house she worked so hard to build—that would be something she could never accept. The more she thought about it, the more confused she became about what she should do. In the end, she just locked herself in her room and started to cry—she cried until her eyes swelled up—and she didn't even come out to eat.

She cried so much that night that she ran out of tears and completely exhausted herself. She had no idea how she was going to get through the days ahead. She lay in bed absolutely consumed by frustration.

Yingzhi's mother knocked on the door and called out to her daughter. Yingzhi thought her mother was calling her to eat, so she ignored her out of spite. But then her mother said, "Yingzhi,

Chunhui came back from down south today. She made a special trip here to see you."

"Chunhui?" Yingzhi suddenly sat up in bed. She thought back to what Liu San had told her about Chunhui when they were in Wild Goose Village. The image of Chunhui driving her car through a forest of skyscrapers suddenly flashed through Yingzhi's mind. Ignoring how much her feet hurt, Yingzhi leaped out of bed and rushed over to open the door. Standing there before her was indeed Chunhui. Yingzhi embraced her like a long-lost relative and through her tears said, "Chunhui, is it really you? You're really here!"

Chunhui appeared uncomfortable in Yingzhi's embrace; she pulled herself away, and Yingzhi led Chunhui into her room. Chunhui was still wearing glasses, but this new pair had a gold frame. She was wearing light makeup and a Western-style outfit that made her look like a city person. She asked, "What's going on with you? You never used to be like this."

Yingzhi didn't respond to Chunhui's question. She was still thinking about Chunhui's car and couldn't wait to ask her about it. "I heard you own your own car? How much money do you make a month?"

Chunhui offered a cool smile. "What are you talking about? I haven't even graduated yet."

"Liu San from Wild Goose Village told me you had your own car and treated him to a fancy meal," said Yingzhi.

"Oh, that was when I was working for a company during summer break," explained Chunhui. "I was doing some designs for them. One of the lead designers had made a lot of money and gave me a bonus. The car was my friend's; during our break we drove it around for fun."

Yingzhi didn't believe her and frowned. "Why are you pulling my leg? Are you afraid I'm going to ask you for money?"

Chunhui grew anxious. "Yingzhi, if I was going to pull anyone's leg, it wouldn't be yours! Don't you remember always walking me home from school at night? If you hadn't held my hand, I would have fallen into the river and drowned many times over."

Chunhui's response cheered Yingzhi up. She knew that Chunhui would never lie to her. She also knew that Chunhui would never forget her. That's when she came back to Chunhui's question, which elicited a long sigh.

Seeing her sigh, Chunhui said, "Your mom told me about what you've been through. She said your husband drinks, gambles, and even beats you. He should feel lucky to have married such a beautiful and capable woman like you. How could he ever raise his hand to you? It's unconscionable! If you can't stand it anymore, you should just divorce him!"

Yingzhi felt better knowing that someone was able to see things from her perspective. But she replied, "It's not that easy. I haven't even told my husband that I've been considering a divorce. As soon as I mentioned it to my parents, they practically exploded! My dad even threatened to break my legs! How am I supposed to get divorced when even my own parents are threatening me? On top of that, I put every cent I earned into building a new house, which still isn't finished. If I get divorced, that house will be my husband's property! I can't tell you how frustrating all this has been. I really don't know how I'm going to get through the coming days. I wish I could just kill myself and get it all over with!"

"Don't think those crazy thoughts!" Chunhui tried to encourage her. "It's your life. If you die, at the very most he'll probably just shed a few tears and before long he'll find himself a new pretty young wife. He won't even feel sorry that you're gone. People who end their own lives are the stupidest."

"Chunhui, you've been to college and seen the world. Please tell me, what should I do?" pleaded Yingzhi.

"Given how capable you are and your good looks, you could make it anywhere! No need to hang yourself from some tree! If you don't want to get divorced but also can't stand living with him, just leave! Head south and look for work there. Tons of people from the countryside have managed to make a life for themselves there. They're more open and liberal down in the south. You'll be much happier working there than in this backward, closed-off village!"

As Chunhui spoke, in Yingzhi's mind it was as if a lightbulb turned on, flooding the dark corners of her heart with light. Yingzhi wondered why she hadn't thought of that idea before. *If I can no longer stand it here, why shouldn't I just leave? How wonderful it would be if I could set out to see the colorful world that awaits out there! Otherwise, what's the purpose of this life of mine? To just sit here raising Jianhuo and taking their insults for the rest of my life? How could that be worth it?*

Just thinking about the possibility excited Yingzhi. She asked Chunhui, "Are you serious? Is working down in the south really that good?"

"There are tens of thousands of people down there doing just fine! Even people with cross-eyes and crooked noses manage to find work there, so how could someone like you not find a good job? If you ask me, you'll be wasting your life if you don't get out of here and see what the outside world is like! You can't just spend your life holed up in that village!"

Yingzhi replied, "You're right! You're exactly right! I don't want to waste my life anymore!"

Yingzhi and Chunhui stayed up talking until the middle of the night. Chunhui promised to ask around to see if there were any jobs that might be appropriate for Yingzhi. She said she would send a letter as soon as she had news, and Yingzhi could then come out. Chunhui even wrote out on a scrap of paper which train to take, where to get off, and how to get in touch with her once Yingzhi arrived. Yingzhi had never been on a train in her life, as there weren't any train lines out in the plains area where she lived; she had seen a train only a few times when she was visiting Hankou. Chunhui told her that if she wanted to get a job down south, she would have to board the train at Hankou and it would take a whole day and night to get there.

Yingzhi clasped that scrap of paper close to her chest and told Chunhui, "This paper is like a lucky charm that's going to save my life!"

After Chunhui left, Yingzhi felt as if her choked-up heart was finally released; her entire body relaxed, and her stomach finally started to grumble after having skipped so many meals. She went into the kitchen, lit up the stove, and cooked herself a big pot of noodles. Against the faint light from the stove, she ate three bowls of noodles, finishing everything in the pot. She was so bloated after eating that she kept passing gas.

Before dawn, Yingzhi's father was on his way out to the fields driving an ox when he ran into Guiqing. Guiqing was on his bicycle, and as soon as he saw Yingzhi's father, he anxiously hopped off his bike and said, "Dad, you're going out to the fields again?"

Yingzhi's father didn't directly answer his question; instead, he just slowly said, "You need to realize that Yingzhi is a human being. You knew that she walked home in the middle of the night. How come you didn't give her a ride on your bicycle? Instead, she walked home barefoot, tearing up the soles of her feet!"

That's when Guiqing realized that Yingzhi had left without out shoes. He immediately felt terrible. He didn't know how to respond. But Yingzhi's father didn't stop; he just continued driving his ox forward. He took a few more steps before turning to say, "You have to have a reason for hitting your wife. What kind of man hits his wife for no reason? If she ends up leaving you, do you really think you'll be better off? By the time you get to my age, you'll realize that without a wife you're no better than a dog."

Guiqing tried to explain, "I didn't hit her this time, she hit me!"

But Yingzhi's father replied, "You took all the money she borrowed and gambled it away. She was right to hit you. Don't tell me you didn't deserve it."

With that, Yingzhi's father urged his ox forward and went off into the distance. He left Guiqing standing there dumbfounded. It was quite some time before Guiqing finally cursed, "So when I hit her, she doesn't deserve it, but when she hits me it's justified? Fuck that!"

Yingzhi was still asleep when Guiqing entered her bedroom. Chunhui's idea had gotten Yingzhi so worked up that she couldn't get to sleep for half the night. Yingzhi was the kind of person that dreamed many dreams, and that night her dreams were filled with images of trains. She rode one train after another. The trains roared through the green plains, their rumbling shaking the earth and reverberating through the sky. Guiqing noticed that Yingzhi's feet, which were sticking out from under her blanket, were both wrapped in bloodstained towels and that some of the blood had hardened into little clumps. Guiqing knew that those bloodstains were from her walking home barefoot the previous night. He thought, *What's the point of picking a fight with me and then wearing your own feet out like that?* It was at that moment that Yingzhi started smiling about something in her dream. Guiqing was mystified by that smile. He wondered, *I lost all your money gambling, and you scratched up my face. What's there for you to be so happy about?*

XIV

As they slowly strolled alongside the river, they noticed the willow trees forming a canopy over the river, their branches drooping all the way down to the water's surface. The green grass was no longer flattened out on the ground and with the changing seasons had sprouted up high, creating a thick layer of foliage covering the river bank. The mud path through the grass created by the foot traffic of farmers and their oxen shone brightly.

Guiqing pushed his bicycle along that shiny path at a leisurely pace. Sitting on the frame of his bike was Yingzhi, her feet wrapped in a floral-patterned cloth. At first Yingzhi refused to sit on the bike; she stubbornly said, "I'll go back on my own two feet, the same way I came!" But Guiqing sneered, "Yesterday when you hit me, I didn't hit back; and now today I rode all the way out to pick you up and you're refusing me? C'mon, give me a break here!"

Yingzhi silently snorted, thinking, *You gambled away every cent of that 3,000 yuan and you think this is the end of it?* But then she figured there was really no point in continuing to give him a hard time.

Since it was late morning, hardly anyone was out on the path. All the cattle herders and day laborers were already out in the fields, and the idlers were all back in the village playing mah-jongg. No one ever came out here just to enjoy the scenery. Devoid of people, the scenic path was so peaceful and quiet that it almost felt as if you could hear the sound of the flowers blooming and the grass growing. As soon as Guiqing's bicycle turned onto that dirt path, Yingzhi's mood immediately lightened. She stopped nagging Guiqing about the money he had lost and started chatting about some unrelated topics. There was a relaxed joy to their conversation, as if this were their first day together and none of those other things between them had ever happened. As they followed the path along the river, it was as if they were falling in love for the first time. Guiqing was a bit confused, even somewhat timid; he knew that Yingzhi was not easy to deal with, and he wondered if another round of fiery attacks was imminent.

Naturally, Yingzhi had her own ideas. She kept her cards close to her chest, for she knew exactly what Guiqing meant to her. She felt that her only path forward now was to go to work down south. For her and Guiqing to continue to live under the same roof with her in-laws in Old Temple Village would be a fate worse than death. Yet she was too scared to seek out a new life by herself; she decided the best option would be for Guiqing to go with her. Once they were away from his parents, how could he not listen to her? And once Guiqing started working in a factory, even if he wanted to slack off, he'd have no choice but to do the same job as everyone else. Once her in-laws were old and dead and the two of them had spent enough time away from home, they could return to the village and live a quiet life. Yingzhi thought she had come up with the perfect little plan.

The scenery along the river might have been gorgeous, but it never changed. Guiqing also wasn't someone who had the ability to admire natural scenery. Moreover, the woman beside him wasn't an exciting new lover; she was his wife, and he was already growing weary of her. Guiqing said, "Aren't you getting tired of continuing along this path? Let's go up to the main road."

Yingzhi was also getting tired, but she insisted on always opposing what her husband said, so she answered, "Who's tired? The scenery is beautiful, and it's rare that the two of us have quiet time alone like this. My classmate Chunhui told me that couples in the city walk around holding hands! Even when there is no scenery, they still really enjoy taking walks together—she said the city folk call that 'going for a stroll'!"

Guiqing laughed. "Who does she think she is? Who are we? We're all peasants! If a peasant walked down the road holding his wife's hand, everyone in the village would laugh their teeth out! Any man who did that would be a laughingstock!"

"That's because peasants are backward," said Yingzhi. "In the city, all the men know how to make their women happy. They defer to the ladies on everything. At least that's what Chunhui said. According to her, that's what it means to be civilized."

"That sounds weird to me. So allowing your women to take advantage of you on everything is what it means to be civilized? If that's the case, then what do men need that for? I for one don't want it!" exclaimed Guiqing.

"Try to be a little more open-minded! Why don't you go south for yourself to take a look? You can see how men behave down there," suggested Yingzhi.

Guiqing burst out laughing. "What the hell would I go there for? What good would it do you if I went down south? Haven't you heard? All those men down south have mistresses. You want me to find myself a mistress too?"

Yingzhi grew testy. "Anytime I say something, you always twist it in the filthiest ways! Don't you want to go south to see how all those men make the big bucks?"

"Yingzhi, you need to stop dreaming. No matter how much money I make, I'll never become the richest man in China. Hell, I don't think I'll even ever become the richest man in Old Temple Village! There are always people out there with more money than you, and you'll always be comparing yourself to them, so what's the point? Besides, Old Temple Village isn't that poor; we all live decent lives there. Why would I leave home only to endure all that suffering? It'd be like signing my own death warrant!" argued Guiqing.

Guiqing thought, *So you took me out here beside the river so that you could ask me to move down south to get a job and earn more money! I'm just fine right here in the village. I get to have fun when I want to and I work when I feel like it. If I move down south, I'll have to work nonstop and be constantly worried about pleasing my boss! Does she think I'm crazy?*

Yingzhi was once more angry and frustrated. She just didn't understand why Guqing had so little ambition. "I don't understand why you're not willing to work a bit harder," she said. "You think you have a great life? You built half a house and ran out of money to finish it! How great is that?"

As Guiqing had suspected, his wife finally steered their conversation back to the topic of the money needed to finish their house. He was curious to hear how she planned on dealing with this problem, so he said, "It's not like we don't have a place to live! We can always finish the house later once we have some money."

But that only upset Yingzhi more. Not even the wonderful plan that Chunhui had laid out for her could stop her from losing her temper. Yingzhi responded angrily, "Later, later, later! What do you mean by later? You think I just found that money lying on the ground? You think I don't need to return it? As you were gambling all the money away, did you ever stop to think about all the blood and sweat your wife expended earning that money? And when it wasn't enough, I even swallowed my dignity and asked others for a loan to get the rest! Did you even think about any of that?"

"What's there to think about?" replied Guiqing matter-of-factly. "When you gamble you win some, you lose some. I had a run of bad luck and ended up losing. So what are you saying, I shouldn't pay my debts? You should know that gambling debts must always be repaid!"

Yingzhi burst out in anger. "Wow, you have the gall to make excuses for yourself! Have you ever thought about not gambling?"

Guiqing lashed back. "If I don't gamble, what the hell am I supposed to do? Don't tell me I should start stripping off my clothes and singing for people, like you?"

Yingzhi wanted to slap her husband upside the head, but she knew that taking a hard line with him wouldn't work. Guiqing was no pushover, and if things escalated, she would be the one who would suffer. And so she suppressed her temper in order not to blow up her big plan over some small details. Her main objective wasn't to get in a fight with Guiqing; she was trying to find a way to move south. That was now the place of her hopes and dreams.

Yingzhi gritted her teeth and suppressed all the terrible things she wanted to say to Guiqing. She adopted a cool and composed tone and simply said, "There's no point in going on arguing with you. I'm now in debt and I have to pay that money back. If you're not willing to go out and earn that money, then I will."

Guiqing perked up. "Great! I knew that you'd have a plan on how to earn that money back. If you want to go out to make some money, I promise to support you 100 percent!"

Yingzhi was taken aback by her husband's response. "Really? You'll really support me?"

"Of course! How could I not? If you want to be my personal cash cow, what's not to support? As long as you don't prostitute yourself, do whatever the hell you want!"

Yingzhi felt relief. "All right then, I'll leave next month."

"Leave?" Guiqing was confused. "Where are you going?"

"I'll head south to find a job. So many people are going south to make money. My old classmate Chunhui is already down there. She's going to help me find a job," explained Yingzhi.

Guiqing hollered, "Stop messing with me! After all that beating around the bush, your plan all along was to pack up and hit the road! You think I'm a stupid child? If you want to stay here and get a job to make money, I promise to fully support you. But you're crazy if you think I'm going to let you leave! You don't think I know what most women do to earn money when they are down south?"

Yingzhi instantly knew what her husband was implying, but she had no idea how to respond to him. So she just stammered, "You . . . you . . . you . . . Why do you have to be like that?"

"That's just who I am! I don't give a rat's ass about most things, but when it comes to who gets in my wife's pants, you better believe that I'm gonna have a say! I'm keeping that under lock and key! I'm afraid that not one penny earned down south is clean money!" declared Guiqing.

Yingzhi was at a loss as to what to say to Guiqing. She decided to remain silent. She hopped off the bicycle, lowered her head, and just started walking by herself. The pain was excruciating when she first put pressure on her feet, but after taking a few steps, she felt that she could handle it. Her pace quickened as she walked, as if her quickly shifting mood were driving her pace. The scenery beside the river seemed to be changing colors before her eyes.

Walking his bike, Guiqing tried to catch up to her, shouting, "Hey, what are you walking so fast for? Are you rushing off to the crematorium?"

Yingzhi impatiently shouted back, "Your house isn't much better than a crematorium! Let me make this clear, Guiqing: if you really insist on acting this way, there is no way we can continue living together!"

"Okay, okay!" Guiqing relented. "Just take it as a joke, okay? What exactly is it that you want?"

"The way I see it, there are only two options: either your parents cough up the money we need to finish our house or I'll go south to find a job. I don't see any other options," said Yingzhi.

"Both of those are going to be difficult. I'm sure my parents won't agree to that first option. They cling to their money like it's as important as life itself! And I'm certainly not going to agree to that second option! There's no way I'm going to allow my wife to leave home for work! Is there a third option?"

"Yes," replied Yingzhi. "Return all the money I gave you to build the new house and then we get divorced."

"Whoa!" Guiqing howled. "This option is even more cruel than the first two! Don't scare me. I hit the jackpot with a wife like you: you're good looking, you know how to make money, and you're great in the sack! How could I ever agree to a divorce?"

"Then I'll leave! I'll walk out of here on my own two feet. I'll go so far away from here that you'll never be able to find me!" Yingzhi declared.

"Stop messing with me, okay? Let's go home and talk it over with my parents. Who knows, maybe they're so fed up with you that they'll be happy to get you out of their sight!"

When Yingzhi heard that she slowed down and said, "And how about you? Are you coming with me or not?"

"Of course I'll go with you!" said Guiqing. "I'd be really screwed if you ended up getting abducted by some other man!" Guiqing caught up with Yingzhi and abruptly stopped. He grabbed hold of Yingzhi by the waist, picking her up, and put her back on his bicycle. He laughed. "But for now, you're going with me!"

On the other side of the river a boy was tending to his bull. When he saw them flirting with each other, he called out a ditty:

"The sun goes up in the east and down in the west,
   That guy's heart burns in his chest.
   Tried to plant one on the girl's face,
   But she said no, what a disgrace!"

Guiqing snickered and cursed, "You little bastard! You may be small, but you've sure got a big mouth on you!"

XV

All summer long Yingzhi kept discussing her plan to go down south with Guiqing. That day by the river Guiqing had agreed to talk it over with his parents, but as soon as they got home, he changed his tune. He figured that since he had already reconciled with his wife, there was now no reason to stir up more trouble with his parents. So he was hesitant to bring it up. Yingzhi was so furious that she started giving Guiqing the silent treatment. It didn't really matter when she ignored him during the day, since he was out playing mahjongg with his buddies, but it was a different story at night. Guiqing couldn't stand going to bed without having someone to talk to before falling asleep, so he pestered Yingzhi and made numerous empty promises. Of course, when the next morning came, all those promises vanished into thin air and he refused to discuss any of Yingzhi's ideas with his parents.

Then one day Guiqing's sister returned home to pick up another installment of money from her parents to cover her living expenses. The whole family was sitting around the table, and seeing his parents in a good mood, Guiqing brought up the idea of going down south with Yingzhi to look for a job. Guiqing's sister, having seen and heard a lot during her time living in town, immediately voiced her approval. She encouraged them to go out there and give it a try; even if they didn't make a lot of money, at least they could see the world. But Guiqing's parents instantly shot down the idea. Guiqing's father said, "I know what happens there. Whenever you hear about factory fires or manufacturing plants collapsing, it is always people from the countryside like us who die. There's not even a body left to bury. You're the only son I've got; you know the old saying 'As long as the parents are still living, the son shan't roam far from home.' You need to stay good and healthy right here at home with us!" As soon as Guiqing's father gave his opinion, his mother immediately echoed his sentiments: "If you stay here at home, everything will be safe and secure and you don't have to worry about things like where your next meal is coming from. What's the point of going so far away and leaving your parents alone here worried sick?" Hearing his parents' reasoning, Guiqing couldn't agree more. Everything was perfectly comfortable here with his parents; they weren't that poor, so why leave home and even take the risk of putting his life in danger? As soon as Guiqing took his parents' side, Yingzhi rolled her eyes in frustration. Even Guiqing's little sister criticized him: "You are so damn conservative! It's really pathetic!"

Summer came and all the pears in their orchard were ripe. Although Guiqing's family's pears didn't look pretty, the flesh inside was white and sweet. The whole family was busy harvesting the pears and selling them; Guiqing didn't even have time to go out and play mah-jongg with his friends. With Guiqing working so hard in the orchard, it wasn't convenient for Yingzhi to keep pestering him. Every day Yingzhi would haul the pears that her husband and father-in-law had harvested out to the street to sell. The only reason she agreed to do that was because she made a deal with her husband that half the money they brought in would be set aside for their house. Guiqing gave

the idea his full blessing. That also provided Yingzhi with the
incentive to work hard. Yingzhi was a pretty woman with a nice
crisp voice who also knew how to flirt; as soon as someone took
one look at her pears, she would immediately light up with a
smile. Her charming ways won over quite a few customers on
the street; once she had them in the palm of her hand, they all
reached deep into their wallets to buy her pears. Yingzhi was the
first one on the street to sell all the pears in her basket. None
of the other women selling pears in Old Temple Village could
even compare. But secretly the other girls all gossiped behind
her back, saying that she wasn't selling pears, she was selling her
good looks! When Yingzhi got word of what they were saying,
she wasn't at all upset; in fact, she was a bit proud. She thought,
*No matter what product you're selling, the appearance of the per-
son selling it is always part of the package. If you aren't pretty, who
would ever want to buy your stuff?*

In the blink of an eye it was already autumn. The pears had
all been sold, and Guiqing gradually stopped going out to the
orchard as frequently. As soon as the weather started to cool
down, all the young guys in the village went back to their old
ways, endlessly playing mah-jongg. During her downtime waiting for customers, Yingzhi had been knitting a pair of pants for
Jianhuo. Now that she no longer had to go out to market, she
took a day to finish her knitting. Once that was done, she turned
her attention back to her house. Yingzhi's plan was to complete
the house during the autumn and winter and then head south
right after Chinese New Year. Chunhui wrote her a letter telling
her that the best time to find work was right after the Spring
Festival holiday. All the money that Guiqing had gambled away
belonged to Wentang. She knew that she could never rely on
Guiqing to return that money; at the end of the day, she would
have to rely on herself.

One night after dinner, just as Guiqing was getting ready to go out to play mah-jongg, Yingzhi called him over. She said, "Now that all the pears have been sold, have you split the money up with your parents yet?"

"I gave it all to them! How could I ask for it back now?" said Guiqing.

Yingzhi exploded the second she heard that. "We already agreed that half the money was to be set aside for our house! Why can't you ask for it back?"

"When I gave my dad the money, I tried to explain it to him, but my mom said that all this time they've been taking care of Jianhuo and haven't asked for one cent. Also, the three of us have been eating at home and have never contributed to the food bill. So they decided to keep all the money. It's actually less than what we really owe them for all that food and rent."

"What!" screamed Yingzhi. "Do you mean to tell me that I worked my ass off selling these pears all summer and now I'm not seeing one cent of that money?"

"You can't look at it like that. Every day we are at home and there are all kinds of expenses for food, drinks, and all the various things we use. That stuff isn't free! What's more, the pear orchard is basically my dad's; we just help him out during the harvest season when it's time to sell the fruit. Taking half the profits doesn't really make sense," explained Guiqing.

Yingzhi began to tremble with anger. She smashed the teapot that was on the table. Seeing his wife starting to act up, Guiqing worried she might prevent him from making it to his mah-jongg gathering. He quickly raised his voice to say, "I'm trying to talk sense to you! What the hell are you losing your temper about?" With that, he rushed out the door.

Yingzhi continued trembling and even screamed for a while, but the house was empty and no one was there to argue with her. That was when Jianhuo came inside looking for his mother. Yingzhi took a deep gulp, grabbed hold of Jianhuo, and began spanking her son. Jianhuo cried, wailing until his face was covered with tears and snot. Yingzhi's in-laws rushed in cursing as the pulled their grandson away from Yingzhi.

After having been spanked for absolutely nothing, Jianhuo kept screaming at the top of his lungs, filling the room with his cries. As his grandparents consoled him, they also cursed Yingzhi and said some rather unsavory things about her. Hearing the combination of Jianhuo's pathetic wailing and her in-laws' vicious attacks, Yingzhi was beside herself. In the end, she threw herself onto her bed and broke down crying. Through her tears she thought, *Since things have come to this and there is no hope of ever finishing that house, I may as well leave now. I should get as far away from this place as I can and never again in my life come back!*

After letting all her tears out, Yingzhi thought, *Never again will I shed as many tears as I have on this day.*

The next morning Yingzhi quietly packed up her things. She figured that she would never get Guiqing's consent if she told him what she was about to do. She asked herself, *Would I still go if Guiqing refused to let me? Why do I always need to get his approval for everything I do? When did he ever ask for my consent for anything he ever did? If I'm really done with him being my husband, then what they hell do I need his consent for? It's my life and I'll lead it the way I want. Who cares about Guiqing?* Thinking about it like that, Yingzhi had no misgivings.

Yingzhi packed her clothes and other articles in a small bag, which she hid under the bed. She planned to visit her parents before she left. She just wanted to see them one last time before setting out because she had no idea when she would have a chance to see them again. But she didn't intend to tell her parents about her plan to go south—that would be like selling herself out.

Yingzhi figured that now that things had reached this point, there was no reason for her to say too much. Once she had settled in the south and earned a ton of money, her parents would surely forgive her when she came home and showered them with cash.

Now that she had a plan, Yingzhi felt extremely calm. She carried Jianhuo on a leisurely stroll around the village. After having been spanked for no reason, Jianhuo eventually stopped crying and almost immediately forgot why he'd been upset in the first place. His two little hands clung tightly to Yingzhi's neck as he giggled away in her arms.

Yingzhi set Jianhuo down on the ground near the village entrance. She watched him run off to play with a dog. That's when she suddenly wondered if her departure meant that she would eventually become a stranger to Jianhuo. As Jianhuo played with the dog, he kept muttering, "Mommy, mommy, mommy," like a little baby. It took only those cries of "mommy" to soften Yingzhi's hardened determination to leave everything behind. She asked herself, *Do I really want to leave?*

Deep down, Yingzhi felt so confused. She picked up Jianhuo to go home, but her son kept saying that he wanted to play some more with the doggy. Yingzhi was still trying to get Jianhuo to come home when she noticed someone far off in the distance approaching. Something about the person's silhouette looked familiar, and so she kept an eye on him. As he got closer, Yingzhi's heart started to pound as if it were about to leap out of her chest. The first thing that crossed her mind was that 3,000 yuan she had put in that pocket against her belly, then she thought about what she had done in that small private room at Tap Dance . . . the man approaching was Wentang.

Wentang walked straight up to Yingzhi and laughed. "What's wrong? It's only been a few months since I saw you last and you've already forgotten about me?"

Yingzhi giggled. "How could I forget? Even if you were burned to ash, I'd still recognize you!"

"Okay, as long as you know who I am," replied Wentang. "Is this your son? So when you got married, this is the little bastard you were pregnant with?"

"Hey, watch your mouth! He is my proper son I had with Guiqing. He's not a bastard!" objected Yingzhi.

Wentang scanned the area to make sure no one else was around before offering a snide remark. "If I had knocked you up last time, we would have had our own little bastard together!"

Yingzhi couldn't help but laugh at his joke.

"So is your new house finished?" asked Wentang.

Yingzhi still had a smile on her face from Wentang's rude joke, but the second she heard him ask about the house her expression changed. She heaved a deep sigh. "Everything would have been great if it was . . ."

"What happened?" asked Wentang. "Not enough money?"

Yingzhi's eyes grew red as she explained, "The day after you loaned me the money, Guiqing went out to purchase the remaining building supplies. But instead . . . he gambled it all away in a single day. He lost every cent."

Wentang was visibly shocked. "He lost all three thousand!"

Yingzhi nodded. Wentang asked, "How could your husband do such a thing? That's not the kind of thing any decent person would do!"

"What recourse do I have? I had a big fight with him about it, but what good did that do me? He just keeps gambling like before. He's at the mah-jongg table right now," said Yingzhi.

"My God, this must have been so fucking hard on you!" exclaimed Wentang. "Yingzhi, you should just divorce him! Are you afraid you won't find someone else?"

"You think it's that easy?" asked Yingzhi. "Forget it. I don't want to talk about it. So, what brings you to Old Temple Village? By the way, I'm sorry I still haven't returned the money I borrowed from you. But I promise I'll eventually pay you back."

Wentang sighed. "My wife is in the hospital, and business at the club has been slow. Originally, I came out here to see if you could at least pay back the first thousand. But since it seems you're having a hard time too, don't worry about it."

"Thank you, Wentang," said Yingzhi.

"But then again . . . it wouldn't be good if I came all the way out here for nothing, now would it? As Wentang spoke he gazed at Yingzhi with a flirtatious smile.

Yingzhi blushed. "Then what do you want?"

Wentang lowered his voice and looked into Yingzhi's eyes. "What do you think?"

The way Wentang was looking at her excited Yingzhi; she could feel the blood pulsating through her body. She figured that since she had to go through the county seat to take a long-distance bus to Hankou anyway, she might as well go home tonight to see her parents; then she could stay at Wentang's place the following night before leaving for good. She figured that if she took really good care of Wentang, he might even give her some pocket money for the road. Otherwise, she would have only enough money for her train ticket. After thinking it through, she decided her plan was flawless. It was as if Wentang had suddenly dropped from the sky just in time to help her.

"If I go off with you today, Guiqing will surely find out and he'll kill me! I was going to visit my parents' house tomorrow. Why don't I go from there to your place?" suggested Yingzhi.

After thinking about it, Wentang liked the plan. He laughed. "Then it's a date! But don't keep me waiting. I think I'd go crazy if you kept me waiting for more than one night!"

Yingzhi also laughed. "Got it. I'll show you a good time tomorrow night!"

As they talked and laughed, Yingzhi headed in the direction of home. Just before they arrived at the front gate, she warned, "My in-laws are really suspicious people. If they see me bringing you home, they're sure to start talking trash about it."

"So you want to send me off without even offering me a drink? No matter what, I did lend you 3,000 yuan to finish construction on your house!" protested Wentang.

Yingzhi thought about it and said, "Okay, how about I take you out to see the construction site for the new house? Wait for me here while I take Jianhuo inside. I'll bring you something to drink. I'll just tell my in-laws that you came to check out the new house."

Wentang sighed and said, "Yingzhi, I never imagined that such a bold and capable woman like you would end up tiptoeing around because you were so afraid of your husband's family! You don't even feel comfortable enough to have an old friend over? Instead you're acting all paranoid as if you're trying to have an affair or something!"

Yingzhi knew that Wentang was right, but she didn't want him to see just how bad a situation she was really in. She adopted a carefree attitude and smiled before saying, "So you're *not* trying to have an affair with me? You're just an 'old friend'? Yeah, that sounds right!"

Her sarcasm made Wentang laugh. From there, he followed Yingzhi out to the construction site. Wentang sat down on the front stoop of the new house to wait for Yingzhi's return. He was a carefree person, and the fact that Guiqing's parents were home didn't seem to bother him in the least; he just sat there staring up at the clouds and whistling. The sound of his whistles was bright and clear, twisting with the wind, and it seemed if the clouds above had extended their hands down to usher each note far off into the sky. Those graceful clouds reminded Wentang of the way in which Yingzhi moved her body when they were together in that private room at Tap Dance. He became excited and was on the verge of losing control.

Yingzhi returned with tea for Wentang, but he didn't realize she was back until she stood right there in front of him. She commented, "Just zoning out looking at the clouds? I brought you some tea; it's a new variety they just came out with this season."

Wentang got up, but he didn't take the tea; instead, he grabbed Yingzhi by the waist. It came as such a surprise that she spilled half the tea on the ground. She exclaimed, "Have you gone mad? If Guiqing finds out he'll kill the both of us!"

"He wouldn't dare! He doesn't care about you—that's why you found me. How can a woman live without someone to love her and care for her?"

Wentang's words brought tears to Yingzhi's eyes. Her entire body relaxed, and she let the teacup in her hand fall to the ground. The cup clanked as it rolled around on the ground. The tea leaves fell everywhere. Yingzhi collapsed into his arms.

Surrounded by silence, the two of them immediately forgot about everything around them. Wentang was so worked up that he wanted more than just fondling. He whispered to Yingzhi, "I'm so hot right now. If you threw a match on me, I'd burn up. You're that match!"

"We can't do it here. We're too close to my in-laws' house. If they catch us, we'll both be done for!" cautioned Yingzhi.

"The new house is empty, and there's no way anybody would be coming. Let's go inside and do it," whispered Wentang.

Thinking it over, Yingzhi realized that Guiqing must still be in the middle of his mah-jongg game, so he certainly wouldn't be coming, and her in-laws were never willing to set foot in the new house. Yingzhi gently nodded.

As Wentang pulled Yingzhi inside, she softly suggested, "Let's go upstairs. It'll be safer there." Fondling and hugging their way up the stairs, the two took a while to finally get up to the second floor. The rooms upstairs were completely empty, and the area where the windows were supposed to go were like two huge open holes, as the window frames hadn't been installed yet. But as far as Wentang and Yingzhi were concerned, neither the empty house nor the lack of windows mattered. In their throes of passion they perceived no such thing as the sun or the air and felt no trace of fear or shame. It was as if they had both gone mad; in that moment all that mattered was their raging bodies. They couldn't wait to get to that place where their bodies would merge into one and, in that moment, it was as if there were nothing in the world to be afraid of.

Their ecstasy was interrupted by the sound of breaking glass. It was the worst timing for something like that to happen, and it immediately startled the two lovers. Their bodies separated. For Wentang it was easy: he just pulled his trousers up while Yingzhi was frantically trying to button up her blouse. She pressed Wentang: "Hurry up and get out of here!" But before Yingzhi could even finish her sentence, they heard someone running up the stairs.

Wentang had no time to say anything. He just rushed out of the room and, instead of taking the stairs, jumped down from the section of the second floor without a railing and scurried off into the forest. He was gone.

Yingzhi's father-in-law stormed up the stairs carrying a long pole. When he appeared in the doorway, Yingzhi still hadn't fixed all her buttons. Her father-in-law howled, "Where is that sleazy man you're sleeping with? Tell him to come out!"

Having been interrupted during the heat of passion, Yingzhi felt as if someone had smashed her bowl just as she was about to dig into a gourmet meal—she was burning with anger. When she saw her father-in-law standing in the doorway with his eyes flaming, she grew even angrier. She thought, *We've been working on this house for months, and you never once came to take a look! And now you come to spy on me! What right do you have to spy on me?* As those thoughts flashed through Yingzhi's mind, she became unhinged. She slowly buttoned up her blouse and looked her father-in-law straight in the eye as she said, "So where is that sleazy man you were talking about? You're the only one here. You're so old, don't tell me you're interested in getting some too?"

Yingzhi's father-in-law was beside himself. He began swinging his pole at Yingzhi. She dodged to the side, and the pole crashed into the corner of the wall, knocking down a chunk of concrete. Yingzhi screamed, "So you're trying to rape me? You think you can even handle me? You're the real sleazy man!"

After screaming like mad, Yingzhi saw her father-in-law frozen with anger. He just stood there heaving, trying to catch his breath; the sight filled her with a strange dread. Quickly changing her attitude, Yingzhi put on a cocky air as she walked straight past her father-in-law and strutted out of the room. From there, she went downstairs and ran straight inside the house. When she reached home, Yingzhi went right into her room and locked the door. She put her hand over her chest as if afraid her heart might leap out. She knew this was going to be her last day at Old Temple Village.

XVI

It wasn't until dusk that Yingzhi's father-in-law finally tracked his son down and dragged him home by his ear. Going all over the village calling for his son, Yingzhi's father-in-law almost lost his voice. But Guiqing wasn't even in the village that day. He was actually across the river attending a wedding at Red Flower Embankment. He went there to drink with Fatty and the rest of his buddies. The village chief's son, Youjie, didn't go because his wife had just given birth. When Youjie heard Yingzhi's father-in-law screaming so desperately, he knew something bad must have happened. Youjie quickly hopped on his bike and rode Yingzhi's father-in-law out to Red Flower Embankment.

As soon as Yingzhi's father-in-law caught sight of his son, he immediately grabbed hold of his ear and dragged him away with absolutely no regard for how such a scene might embarrass him. Guiqing hollered in pain, but his father ignored Guiqing's cries. It was only when they were far enough away from everyone that he finally yelled at Guiqing: "Some man busted into our house and tried sleeping with your wife! And here you are just having a good time! Maybe you don't care about your dignity, but I've got to preserve my face!"

Guiqing kept hollering about how much his ear hurt, and when he heard what his father said about his wife, his first reaction was that his father was blowing things out of proportion. His parents and Yingzhi had by this time become each other's archenemies; they were always exaggerating insignificant things and making a big deal out of nothing. *Yingzhi probably just exchanged a few words with some guy,* Guiqing thought, *but in Dad's mind she was having an affair!* Guiqing quickly replied, "Dad, don't get all wound up. Yingzhi is just a social person. It's no big deal if you saw her talking to another man."

Yingzhi's father-in-law replied, "If she was just talking to another guy, why would she go up to the second floor of your new house with him? Would she need to take off her blouse and rub up against him?"

From the expression on Guiqing's face, it was clear that he was starting to lose his temper. "Is it really necessary for you to talk like that?"

Yingzhi's father-in-law raised his hand and slapped Guiqing across the face and barked angrily at him, "You don't believe what I just told you? But you believe what that shameless bitch says? I saw what happened today with my own eyes! So even if you don't want to trust me, you're going to have to!"

Seeing how worked up his father was, Guiqing finally realized the severity of the situation. He said, "Really? Dad, you witnessed this firsthand?"

Yingzhi's father-in-law explained, "I picked up a big pole and tried to catch them in the act. The guy jumped down from the second floor and ran off into the woods. By the time I got upstairs, that shameless wife of yours was still buttoning up her clothes!" As he spoke, he recalled the things Yingzhi had said to him and his anger overcame his brain. He again grabbed hold of

Guiqing's ear and screamed, "If you don't kill that fucking bitch today, you are no son of mine!"

By the time Guiqing and his father returned home, it was already dark outside.

All the while, Yingzhi was holed up in her bedroom keeping an eye on things. Her clothing was all packed, and she was just waiting for the right moment to sneak out. But her mother-in-law had been in the courtyard gossiping with Youjie's mother for what seemed like forever. Yingzhi could tell that they were talking about her. But Yingzhi didn't care what they said about her—now that things had reached this point, she couldn't care less about any of that. She had already come to terms with her situation; what did she care any longer about maintaining face? The most important thing for her was making sure she had a path forward in life. She needed to stay alive.

The sun set and Youjie's mother finally left. For some reason, Jianhuo was being very fussy, and Yingzhi's mother-in-law brought him into the house. Yingzhi saw that her opportunity had come, so she grabbed her bag, unlocked the door, and made a run for it.

But she was one step too late. As soon as she stepped through the front gate, she caught sight of Guiqing and his father approaching. The two men simultaneously saw Yingzhi, and Guiqing roared, "Where the hell do you think you're going?"

Yingzhi's entire body shuddered. She had just stepped over the threshold and now pulled her leg back inside. Yingzhi knew that there was no escaping what was coming. Just as she stepped back into the courtyard, she saw the lock dangling on the gate and suddenly thought back to the night when she tried to run away only to discover that the front gate was locked. She had an idea: she quickly took the lock off the door and threw it into the pigpen.

Yingzhi then ran back into the house and locked the door to her room. Still concerned they might break the lock, she used her wardrobe to barricade the door. Yingzhi couldn't stop shaking; she didn't know if that was born of fear or anxiety. She was at a loss as to what would happen next. Yet given Guiqing's temper, she knew there was a real possibility that he would beat her to death. Yingzhi was so desperate that she prayed, *God in heaven, please protect me. No matter what happens, please allow me to live. No matter what happens, don't let me die at the hands of Guiqing.*

Before she had even finished her prayer, she could hear Guiqing barking outside her door. He screamed, "Open the door, you dirty bitch! How dare you mess around with another man right here in our own home! Mark my words, I'm going to kill you! How many times have I warned you that if you ever cheated on me, I'd make sure your days would be done for? I'm going to kill you! And I'm going to kill that fucking guy too!"

Yingzhi curled up in her bed. She didn't dare to move or make a sound. Guiqing kept pounding on the door, and the sound of his cursing started to attract the neighbors. That's when Yingzhi heard her husband yelling, "What the hell are you looking at? If you want to see a man beat his wife, go home and watch your father beat your mother!" All the neighbors laughed.

Finally Yingzhi's mother-in-law addressed Guiqing. "Why don't you have dinner first?" she urged him. "You can deal with that bitch after you eat."

Guiqing kicked the door a few more times, then yelled, "You think you can spend the rest of your life hiding out in there? Listen up: I'll starve you to death! If you had any sense, you'd just open the door and come out."

What should I do? What should I do? Yingzhi wondered. *How can I get word to my parents so that they know what's happening? Who could possibly save me during a time like this?* It wasn't hard for Yingzhi to imagine that the end result of all this would be her being starved or beaten to death. Just thinking about her previous beatings at the hands of Guiqing made her entire body burn and ache. *I'd be better off killing myself rather than letting him beat me again like before.* As those thoughts crossed her mind, she looked up at the rafters. The beams were quite thick; it wouldn't be too difficult to hoist a rope up there and hang herself. Yingzhi leaped out of bed, picked up a bedsheet, and started tearing it into strips. She tied the strips together into a rope, pulled a stool over, climbed up, and slipped the rope over one of the beams. She pulled it hard, and it seemed quite sturdy. All she needed to do now was slip her head through the noose, kick the stool away, and it would all be over. The whole process took Yingzhi only a few short minutes. The process of turning a living Yingzhi into a corpse would be even shorter. Her body trembled uncontrollably. It is hard for a person to live in this world, but dying is a simple act. Although life was already meaningless, Yingzhi suddenly wondered why *she* should be the one to die. As if she'd be happy ending her life hanging from the rafters in Guiqing's house in Old Temple Village! She hopped down from the stool. *I'm not going to die today. I only just turned twenty. I still have a long road ahead of me. I know a better life awaits me if I can get out of here. Dying is something I can't accept.* Yingzhi decided, *No matter what, I've got to escape. I must take myself far away from this place and never come back.*

It was just as Yingzhi was going back and forth through all these scenarios in her mind that there was a sudden blackout. The room was thrown into complete darkness. She heard her mother-in-law yell, "Hurry up and light the candles!"

Yingzhi was gripped with excitement, thinking, *God in heaven, have you come to save me?* She quickly moved the wardrobe aside and put her head against the door to hear what she could. Not hearing anything, she quietly unlocked the door. But before she could fully open the door, Guiqing burst in with a stick in his hand. He yelled, "You fucking bitch, I knew you would try to sneak away under the cover of darkness! Keep dreaming!"

Waving that stick above his head, Guiqing rushed toward her. But with the lights out, he couldn't see the wardrobe Yingzhi had moved to block the door in front of him. His stick crashed down on top of the wardrobe, and not having enough time to adjust his attack, Guiqing bashed his head into the wardrobe. "Shit," Guiqing exclaimed as he collapsed to the floor. Meanwhile, Yingzhi slipped out the door from the other side of the wardrobe. When Yingzhi's in-laws heard Guiqing yell, they rushed over to see if he was okay. Lying on the floor, Guiqing exclaimed, "I don't know what that fucking woman has up her sleeve! Hurry up and turn the lights back on. We can't let her get away!"

Everyone in the house started looking for Yingzhi. But in the pitch black she couldn't find the front door; she was so disoriented that she didn't even know which room of the house she was in. Shuddering with fear, she hid behind a door. Guiqing and his parents were searching the house but didn't go into the room where Yingzhi was hiding. Once her eyes adjusted to the darkness, Yingzhi realized she was in her in-laws' bedroom. She knew that her father-in-law always kept his money in one of the drawers of the dresser beside the bed. Yingzhi was completely empty-handed—she didn't even have her bag of clothes—and knew that she would need some money if she escaped. She felt her way to the dresser, opened the drawer, and in the darkness grabbed a stack of bills and stuffed them into her pocket. The flash from a dull light turned on in the hallway shone directly into the room as someone yelled, "Search the place from room to room!" That voice belonged to Yingzhi's father-in-law. Yingzhi frantically scanned the room and discovered that the window was open. She quickly ran over to the window, climbed through, and, keeping low, scurried into the courtyard. When she saw the front gate closed, she shuddered with fear: Could they have found the lock? She ran over to the gate, and her heart leaped for joy when she discovered that it was unlocked. Casting her fate to the wind, she opened the gate and began to run.

Guiqing heard the sound of the gate opening and realized that Yingzhi had already escaped. He screamed, "She made it through the gate!" As he spoke, he grabbed hold of a pole and ran toward the door. As he pursued her, he yelled, "I don't care how far you run, I'll find you, bring you back here, and kill you!"

Yingzhi didn't run far, for she knew that she could never outrun Guiqing. Instead, as soon as she slipped out the front gate, she turned back and ran into their neighbor's courtyard. The neighbor had an outhouse in his courtyard, and she knew that no one would go there so late at night. Yingzhi sneaked inside and squatted behind the wall; she would wait there until the middle of the night and then try to sneak away.

The moon shone above her and a layer of thin clouds floated through the sky. Gazing up at the star-filled night sky, she was struck by how vast and open the heavens appeared. At first Yingzhi had been squatting on the ground, but after a while her legs grew sore and she just sat down on the floor of the outhouse. But even more sore was her aching heart. Looking up again at the boundless sky, she wondered why she had been so lost for her entire life. What led a woman as delicate and beautiful as she was to hide out in a filthy outhouse in the middle of the night? Just thinking about it made her break out in tears. But she made sure to cry silently. To control her sobs, Yingzhi stuck her thumb into her mouth and bit down hard to prevent herself from making even the slightest sound.

Yingzhi had no idea how much time had gone by. The various voices outside gradually quieted down, and one by one, the lights went off in all the windows across the village. Guiqing returned home from his search; he of course went back empty-handed. He complained for a while in the courtyard before eventually going inside. All was quiet. Looking out from a crack inside the outhouse, Yingzhi saw that all the lights were turned off at her in-laws' house. Only then did she slowly stand up and attempt to take a few cautious steps forward. She barely had the courage to leave the outhouse. She made it all the way to the front gate, but then her legs seemed to unconsciously freeze up. Yingzhi silently cursed herself as she thought, *Yingzhi, this is your last chance. If you don't take this opportunity, there won't be another one.*

She pinched her legs so that she could feel the pain and stepped out through the gate. She didn't dare stand up straight for fear that someone would see her, so she walked huddled over, keeping close to the ground.

The bright moon and thin clouds still appeared overhead; all was gentle and quiet on that night. Yingzhi silently slipped out of Old Temple Village.

After leaving the village behind her, Yingzhi stood up straight and turned to gaze back at the outline of Old Temple Village in the distance. She thought, *I will never forget how badly you hurt me. I have no idea which son-of-a-bitch will end up living in the house I built.*

As she walked along the main road toward her parents' house, Yingzhi didn't feel scared. She had walked that same road countless times in the dark before. But after walking for a while, she started to wonder if she was being too conspicuous by walking right there out in the open. What if Guiqing were so angry that he came back out to look for her? He would find her right away.

After thinking about it, she decided it would be safer to stay off the main roads.

As Yingzhi left the main road, she glanced behind her to discover far off under the moonlight a man running toward her. The night was perfectly silent, but Yingzhi could gradually make out the sound of those footsteps on the road behind her. Her heart seemed about to explode as Yingzhi thought she was done for, that it must be Guiqing coming for her. She began to run. In her frantic state, she couldn't tell which way to go; she didn't know what was up ahead and couldn't even see the ground beneath her feet. As she frantically ran, Yingzhi completely forgot about her exhaustion; all she was conscious of was the hiss of the wind blowing against her ears. She ran through a vegetable garden, down a ridge, through a forest, past the coal factory, through an open field, all the way to the edge of a lake. A bed of thick reeds surrounding the lake was whistling and swaying in the wind. Yingzhi waded straight into this sea of reeds. Once in the reeds, Yingzhi disappeared like a grain of sand in the ocean. By then her mind was a complete blank; she didn't realize that she could stop running. And so she used all her remaining strength to push the reeds aside and continue forward. She kept going until she tripped and fell to the ground. Only then did she finally stop running. Yingzhi lay on the ground as if paralyzed, without having the strength to even get up. She thought, *If this is the end, so be it.*

As the lake water gently brushed against the shore, the sound of the waves made its way to Yingzhi's ears. She realized this was Cha Lake—that broad lake filled with lotus flowers. The water in Cha Lake was deep and blue, and you could often see flocks of ducks swimming on its surface. Surrounding Cha Lake were a series of small ponds connected by a network of small streams that all fed into the river. The river near Phoenix Dike, where Yingzhi grew up, was a tributary that came from Cha Lake. But the river water wasn't as clear and pristine as Cha Lake. The water was so polluted that hardly any boats cruised on the river anymore.

Yingzhi lay there motionless amid the reeds for what felt like forever. She couldn't even remember the circumstances that had brought her there. How could she be lying nearly paralyzed in a sea of endless reeds in the middle of the night? She didn't understand where the terror and anxiety that gripped her had come from. The rippling sound of the reeds swaying in the night wind seemed to be responding to the sounds of Cha Lake as the water crashed against the shore. A wild duck quacked as if startled. Gradually, the peaceful and calming sounds of the night soothed Yingzhi's heart. Although she felt as if a century had passed, Yingzhi slowly started to remember everything that had happened. She remembered being curled up like a turtle in that putrid outhouse. She couldn't help crying. She remembered that she could never again go back to Old Temple Village. There was nothing to miss about Old Temple Village or Guiqing. It was even hard for her to feel affection for Jianhuo because she knew he was Guiqing's child.

And what about that unfinished house? It represented many years of hard work for Yingzhi. She had earned it with her singing, her charm, and her body; and one cent at a time, she had saved the money to build it. To earn that money she had sacrificed so much of her self-respect and dignity. She had been forced to take so many insults and slaps to the face. But after all those struggles, she was now left with nothing.

Although Yingzhi had expended the last of her remaining energy on her tears, each wave of her cries was like a gossamer thread of sound swallowed up by the rustling reeds and lapping water. Her cries never reached the expansive sounds of the night. It was if the world were refusing to accept the echoes of her tears.

And then her crying abruptly ceased. She finally realized that crying was of no use to her now. Her tears had never been able to save her. If she wanted to continue living in this world, she needed to start thinking about what to do with the rest of her life.

Yingzhi raised her sleeve to wipe her tears dry. She sat up and began to think about what to do next. The first thing that came to her mind was that she had no money. Then she remembered the money she had taken from her mother-in-law's drawer. She reached into her pocket and pulled out the money. Looking at the bills under the moonlight against the reeds, she discovered they were all small bills each worth less than a yuan. Yingzhi laughed bitterly and was about to throw the bills to the wind, but on second thought she crumpled them up and shoved them back into her pocket. *The next thing I need to do is make some money. Without money, I'll be at the end of my road. I don't even have enough money for a train ticket down south. I can't go back to my parents' house, or Guiqing will find me; my parents will force me to go back to him. Going back to Old Temple Village will be like signing my own death certificate. I'm not afraid of death; it's just that I don't want to die, it's not my time yet. I'm still young. I still have my singing voice, an attractive body, and I have the strength to make enough money to support myself. The next step will be for me to work my ass off so that I can finally build my own house. That house will be my home, and no one will ever be able to drive me away. I'll build it tall, and it will have a toilet and shower, curtains, and even a phone. It'll be every bit as good as those city folks' homes. When I'm finished, I'll show it to Guiqing and his parents just to prove that I don't need them to live a better life than them. After that, I'll start to enjoy my life—a life where I don't have to worry about anyone beating me, cursing me, or rolling their eyes at me. I'll use my own strength and skills as a woman to support myself.*

As Yingzhi kept cycling through those thoughts, the reeds' whistling seemed to bolster her morale. Gradually her thoughts helped her to regain her strength. Her confidence restored a hundredfold, she no longer felt afraid. Anyway, when was she ever afraid? She always did exactly as she pleased!

Yingzhi got to her feet, pushed the reeds aside, and began walking toward the lake.

It was just before dawn when Yingzhi arrived at a small dock beside the lake called Xifen Bay. A small boat was moored beside the dock. Yingzhi sat down at the edge of the water, staring at that boat for a long time. As soon as the first rays of light penetrated the clouds, Yingzhi walked straight toward that boat.

XVII

Three months later Yingzhi left that boat behind. There were three men on the boat, and they all tried to convince her to stay, but their efforts were to no avail. *Wasn't I just trying to make enough money to get myself down south? Why should I keep doing this? What kind of person do they think I am?* Yingzhi had more than 1,000 yuan in her pocket—she had made that money in just three months. During the day she washed clothes and prepared meals for them, and during the night she took turns sleeping with the three men aboard that boat. Her time out on the water was extremely peaceful. But as it grew colder outside, her days on the boat gradually became increasingly empty and lonely. Yingzhi made some calculations and figured she must have saved up more than enough to get her down south, so she decided to return to her parents' house. Her plan was to spend Spring Festival with her parents and then head south together with the other migrant workers from her village after the holiday. There was nothing those three men could do but sit there and watch as Yingzhi got off the boat and left them. She never looked back.

It felt good to be walking on solid ground again. Yingzhi felt as if she had just spent a period of her life in another realm and were now returning home.

Yingzhi went to the county seat, where she bought herself a new red turtleneck sweater and a blue jacket; these she wore to the Tap Dance to visit Wentang. Yingzhi arrived at the Tap Dance club, and just as she was about to ask if Wentang was there, a girl immediately recognized her and came over. "What the hell are you doing coming here?" the girl asked. "Your husband already trashed this place so many times that Wentang had to leave town. He took off for Xinjiang. The new DJ is terrible." She spoke with a tone of disdain.

This news shocked Yingzhi. She had no idea how much had happened while she was out on the river making money. She immediately wondered how things were back at her parents' house in Phoenix Dike.

She rushed home. As soon as Yingzhi stepped through the door, her mother embraced her in tears. Yingzhi's mother cried, "My child, you're still alive?"

Yingzhi could barely wait to ask what happened.

That's when her father interrupted. "I see you remembered that you still have a family? What the hell did you come back for? We'd all be better off if you were dead and they never found your body!"

"What happened? she asked again. "Did Guiqing come around here causing trouble?"

Yingzhi's mother explained, "For a while, he was coming by almost every day. He would always cause a ruckus and accuse us of hiding you. It got to the point where we were living in fear every day. Look, he even burned half the house down. He only stopped coming around and causing trouble this past month after your brother reported him to the police. Your brother reported you missing and told the police you were last seen at your in-laws' house."

Yingzhi looked up to discover that the entire right side of the living room had been burned black; the beams on that side of the ceiling looked like sticks of charcoal. Yingzhi's mother explained that she had been out at the store and Shaoya was the only one at home; if it hadn't been for a few passersby who helped put out the fire, the entire house would have burned down.

Yingzhi was crushed. Thinking about how her situation had affected her family and those around her made her hate Guiqing more than ever. Yingzhi's mother pointed out the gasoline tank that Guiqing had left behind. Yingzhi said, "Okay, if he has the guts to set fire to our house, tonight I will fill this same tank with gasoline and burn his house to the ground!"

Yingzhi's father yelled, "You want to cause more trouble!? Guiqing might be a piece of shit, but you're no angel! You had an affair with another man in *his* house! How could you expect him not to beat you? You disappear into thin air for months at a time. Are you really surprised that he would try to burn your parents' house down? Why don't you go back there like a good girl, apologize, and give him a nice present to make amends? He'll probably scream and yell and knock you around a bit, and after that you just behave yourself and be a good wife!"

Yingzhi's mother wiped away her tears. "Yingzhi, women like us can't do the things you talked about doing. What you proposed doing will only result in you being cursed by the living and forever banished from heaven!"

Hearing how adamantly her parents disagreed with her plan, Yingzhi declared, "If you won't let me go, then you better just give me a bottle of insecticide right now. I'll just kill myself and be done with it all!"

Yingzhi's father replied angrily, "Now you're trying to use suicide to threaten me? If you want to kill yourself, be my guest! But don't you dare make this family lose face again!"

Yingzhi was left frustrated and confused after her parents yelled at her. Already filled with anger and now with her parents yelling at her, she thought, *After all I've been through, why can't you ever try to help me? How come I never feel like my own family is on my side?* In desperation, Yingzhi said, "Okay then, Mom, hand me the insecticide. I'll die right here, right now. Mom, after I'm dead, if you think burying me here in Phoenix Dike is too shameful for the family, just dump my body out in the open fields and let the stray dogs take care of me. But whatever you do, don't let them bury me in Old Temple Village. Mark my words, if I end up buried there, I will come back as a ghost to haunt you!"

Yingzhi's mother grew anxious. "Stop saying such crazy things, Yingzhi! I understand how difficult it's been for you."

Those last words made Yingzhi tear up; she couldn't help breaking down and crying.

That night Yingzhi's brothers and their wives came by to see her. No one asked where she had been for these past few months. They just talked about how great it was to have her back, for now they would have an extra partner to play mah-jongg with.

The sky was particularly bright the next morning. Although the chilly wind accentuated the feeling of cold in the air, the sun was slowly rising. Yingzhi's brothers were going to head over to the county seat to purchase some things for Chinese New Year, and since Yingzhi didn't have anything to do, she decided to go with them.

They all had breakfast together at Yingzhi's parents' house. After they ate, Yingzhi's father went out to mind the shop for his wife. Yingzhi changed into her new outfit. She had originally wanted to spend a few nice days with her family at home for the holidays. But thinking about how things were going, she couldn't help feeling disappointed.

Just before she and her brothers set out, Guiqing approached with a gasoline tank in hand. He had an angry look on his face. Before Guiqing made it to the courtyard, Yingzhi's nephew,

Shaoya, ran in to tell everyone he was coming. Yingzhi's brothers immediately put their food aside and grabbed hold of a rope
and a club. As soon as Guiqing stepped into the courtyard and
was about to start yelling, Yingzhi's two brothers jumped him;
they got him on the ground, turned him over, and tied him up.

Only once Guiqing was tied up did Yingzhi venture outside.
As soon as she laid eyes on him, all her old hatred for him combined with what she had just heard about his behavior. She was
so upset that she started panting for air and couldn't even talk. It
was only after her brothers bound Guiqing to a tree that Yingzhi
was finally able to calm herself down. She walked over to the
tree and kicked Guiqing in the groin. "You bastard! If you have a
problem, you should take it to me. What are you trying to prove
by burning my parents' house down?"

Tied up to the tree, Guiqing struggled. His face turned blood
red as soon as he laid eyes on Yingzhi. She was wearing the new
outfit she had just bought in town; it was a light blue blouse
and skirt with white chrysanthemum patterns. During her
three months on the boat, Yingzhi had spent most of her time
below deck and hardly got any sun; in fact, she now looked even
more pale than before. Filled with jealousy and rage, Guiqing
screamed, "You fucking whore! I really loved you and still you
disrespected me like that! How do you expect me to ever get past
what happened if I don't kill you?"

"You really loved me? How did you love me? You sat on your
ass all day, eating, drinking, whoring, gambling. You gambled
away all the money I worked so hard to earn. You beat me so
hard you nearly killed me! Is that how you show how much you
loved me?" Yingzhi yelled.

"How am I different from any other man in my village? Why
should I have to listen to you? I promised to take care of you
when you're old, and that should've been enough for you. I was

able to look past all the arguments you had with my parents. But how do you expect me to be okay with you fucking around with other men? Am I supposed to just let that go?"

Yingzhi responded, "You know all too well how your parents treated me. My days living under the same roof with them are over. I asked you to get a job and make some money, and you refused. I asked you to borrow some money from your parents and again you refused. I had no choice but to earn all that money myself! How did I earn that money, you ask? Well, let me tell you, I slept with someone to get that 3,000 yuan loan! What do you say to that? At the time you were only too happy to take that money and go spend it!"

Guiqing was so furious that he started struggling to break free. He said, "Even if it kills me, I'm going to fucking chop you up. How can I ever walk in this world with any dignity if I don't kill you?"

"Dignity? You lost that a long time ago! It's too late now," replied Yingzhi. "Because you set fire to my parents' house, my family reported you to the police. The police said that if you ever came back here, they'd arrest you and send you to jail!"

"Yingzhi, what are arguing with him for?" questioned one of Yingzhi's brothers. "Just leave him there baking in the sun; I'll call the police."

"Mom, prepare lunch for the police officers. Let's give them a good meal before they take this fucking animal to prison!" said Yingzhi.

Guiqing and Yingzhi were the only two left in the courtyard. Guiqing was panting for breath. Seeing him struggling to breathe made Yingzhi pity him a little. She thought as long as he agreed to a divorce, there was no reason to be at war with his family; after all, there had been times when Guiqing was good to her. Yingzhi thought about it and proposed, "Actually, I could ask the police to release you. But I have two conditions. First, you must agree to a divorce. Since things have already come to this, what would be the point of us being together, anyway? Second, all the money I earned that was spent on the house and your gambling debts adds up to at least 10,000 yuan. I don't want it all back, but I think you owe me at least half. Does that sound reasonable? If you agree to these two terms, I'll speak to the police on your behalf and ask them to release you. Think about it. It's a better deal than going to jail."

"You shameless bitch! Don't you ever think of running away from me again! I'm going to strangle you right there in our bed. And don't you ever dream of getting any of that money back. If you want money, you can slave away for my family for the rest of your life, and when you're old, it'll all be yours!" spouted Guiqing.

Guiqing's response left Yinzhi without a shred of the pity she'd had for him a few moments earlier. She flashed him a cold smile. "Keep dreaming. I'm never going back to you. I tried to offer you a way out, but if you don't want it, so be it. You'll get what you deserve."

"That's right, I deserve it! It's all my fault! It's my fault that my wife fucked around with another man! It's my fault that my wife wants to send me to jail! You are so utterly shameless that I don't know how you are even able to look at yourself in the mirror and go on living."

"So what if I'm shameless? You forced me down this path! You beat me like I was some stray dog on the street. I was forced to do whatever I could to get away from you. What dignity do I have left? Every day I was forced to endure your parents' humiliating comments and constant belittling of me. Where was my dignity then? So let me tell you where I've been for the last three months: I've been shacked up every day with a bunch of men!

And every night I told myself I was doing it to spite you! Since you refuse to treat me with any decency, I as Guiqing's wife went out to fuck other men and give them pleasure!"

Guiqing exploded in anger, shaking the trunk of the tree as he franticly tried to break free. But the rope was too tight, and Guiqing was unable to free himself. The anger contorted his face into something hideous. He said, "Do you really think you can evade retribution? Well, Yingzhi, let me tell you, you will face retribution for your actions!"

"Retribution from you? Your father? Your mother? You'll be in prison. Do you think they'll have time to worry about me? You wish!" retorted Yingzhi.

Guiqing roared, "Even if they send me to prison, how many years do you think they'll keep me there? As long as I get out one day, I'll come for you and your entire family! I'll kill every one of you and cut off your family line!"

Yingzhi flashed Guiqing a fierce stare. "You wouldn't dare!"

Guiqing continued to roar back at Yingzhi. "There's nothing I wouldn't do! There's no way I'll spend more than a decade in prison. I promise you that within ten years, there won't be anyone from your family left alive in this world. You dirty bitch, I'll make sure there isn't the faintest stench left of you anywhere on this planet! Even if you run away to the ends of the earth, I will find you and skin you alive, one piece of flesh at a time! I'll feed you to the dogs, the pigs, the donkeys, the horses, the chickens, the ducks, the toads, the worms, and every other creature in this world. If you don't believe me, just wait and see! I'm a man of my word!"

By the time he got to the end, Guiqing's words started to turn into a series of howls; he sounded like a wolf in the mountains. Those howls made their way over the roof of Yingzhi's house and all the way out to the garden in the back. Yingzhi's mother was out in the garden picking vegetables when she heard his animal-like howls. Startled, she called over, "What's happening? Don't let him get away!"

"Mom, just let us deal with him," Yingzhi called back.

"Anyway, I'm going to pick up some soy sauce," said Yingzhi's mother. "But you better stop squabbling with him. Just let the police deal with him."

Guiqing started to laugh like a madman. "That's right, let them deal with me! Let them take me away! How long do you think I'll be away? When I come back in a few years, I'll tear your family apart from its very roots!"

Yingzhi couldn't stop shuddering as a feeling of intense terror welled up inside her. Shaoya and Chrysanthemum, her nephew and niece, were chasing each other around playing. The sound of their laughter made its way into the courtyard and right up to Yingzhi's ears: *Ding dong, ding dong*, sounding like a ringing silver bell. The sound seemed to suddenly drive away all Yingzhi's fears and injected her with the urge to do something. She wasn't sure what that was, but she could feel that urge burning through her entire being. The burning made it impossible for her to stand, impossible to sit, impossible to speak; it drove her to pace around the courtyard so quickly that everything turned blurry. She wondered what she should do. But what did she want to do? *What did she want?* She kept asking herself that question, but she was still beside herself.

Yingzhi was so anxious that she began to pull her hair, and then she caught sight of the gasoline tank that Guiqing had brought with him with the intention of burning down her parents' house; it was an even bigger tank than the one he used last time. All Yingzhi's anxiety and jumbled thoughts suddenly coalesced into a single idea. It was a firm, solid idea: *If you really dare to do what you keep saying you're going to do, do you really*

think I can let you live? As long as you are living in this world,
will there ever come a day when I am really able to truly free myself
from this misery? And now my entire family must perish because
of you? Oh Guiqing, as long as you live, part of me will always
be dead and my entire family will never be safe. So why shouldn't
I just kill you first?

Yingzhi rushed over and picked up the tank. She unscrewed
the cap and doused the gasoline all over Guiqing's body. All the
while Guiqing carried on with his crazed laughter. "You dare
murder your own husband? Do you really think you'll be able
to go on living if you kill me? You think you'll be able to fuck all
the men you want once I'm dead? You're going to be buried alive
right alongside me!"

Yingzhi responded in kind with a crazed howl. "Whether I
die is none of your damn business. But it all ends today for you!"

After dousing him with the gasoline, Yingzhi looked all over
for a match. Then she remembered that Guiqing was a smoker.
She pounced on him and began frantically searching his pockets.
Since Guiqing couldn't move his body, he headbutted Yingzhi
as soon as she got close enough. But that only drove Yingzhi
further into her state of unhinged madness. She finally found a
box of matches in one of his pockets, and without even thinking, she lit up a match and threw that burning match directly at
Guiqing. As the match left her hand, Yingzhi saw the shock in
Guiqing's eyes. His eyes seemed to be saying, *You really did it?*

It was as if Yingzhi hadn't fully realized what she had done
when the sudden whoosh of flames rose up before her. Guiqing
was transformed into a fireball. From the fire she could hear
Guiqing's screams; his shrill wails were unlike anything she had
ever heard.

Yingzhi stood there in shock. She never imagined that this
would be the end.

As Yingzhi stood there staring in disbelief at what she'd done, the ropes suddenly snapped and that fireball separated from the tree trunk. A red burning beast hurled itself directly at Yingzhi. Shaoya, who had been playing outside, came into the courtyard when he heard the screams. When he saw Yingzhi standing there in shock, he cried out to her, "Auntie, run! Run!"

Yingzhi snapped out of her daze and dashed out of the courtyard. The little dirt road outside the courtyard, which went all the way out to the edge of the village, was flanked by various houses, trees, and vegetation, and roaming around on it were chickens and stray dogs. The sun was already out, and the shadows from several families' courtyard walls projected out into the road. But Yingzhi didn't see any of that as she ran down that road. Chasing right behind her was a ball of fire burning bright. It shot past like a shooting star, blinding like the glare of the summer sun, and more ferocious than a wild animal hurtling down a mountain. Yingzhi could feel the heat emanating from the fire as it came roaring close enough for her to feel it searing her back.

With flames burning every part of his body, Guiqing screamed like mad. He had only one target, and that was Yingzhi. Yingzhi was like a blue butterfly fluttering back and forth before Guiqing's eyes. Those erratic fluttering motions left Guiqing frustrated. How he so wanted to catch her! He screamed, "Stop running! Stop running!" his voice becoming increasingly strange and distorted.

Not knowing who was screaming, people from the village started coming out to see what was happening. One of the villagers shrieked in terror, but most of them stood frozen in shock. No one knew what to do. Yingzhi's hair was all disheveled from her running and her shoes had fallen off; she knew that she couldn't continue much farther. She tried to yell for help but had no strength to make a sound. As she thought back to that night three months earlier when she first ran away, she reflected, *If I had known I'd end up getting burned alive today, I should have just let him kill me back then.*

Yingzhi was on the verge of collapsing. That's when someone rushed over to stop Guiqing. Although Guiqing's eyes were almost burned out, he just kept following the dark shadow he perceived before him. He grabbed hold of that shadow and in a barely discernable voice muttered, "Yingzhi, you'll never escape . . ." As those words left his lips, he fell to the ground. That shadow he embraced fell to the ground with him, screaming in terror.

Someone yelled, "Quick, fetch some water! Douse them with water!"

The fire was extinguished within a few minutes. Guiqing's body looked like a blackened charcoal-like figure. The person he had collapsed on was still screaming in agony. One of the villagers turned the body over, but the face was already unrecognizable. The person's hand was clutching a bottle of soy sauce. It was only when Shaoya showed up that he cried out, "That's my grandma! I recognize her shoes."

But Yingzhi didn't know about any of that. She kept running. She ran all the way to the village public security office, where she collapsed outside the door.

When Yingzhi awakened, she thought she was blind; the only thing before her eyes was that wavering flame. She started to cry. No matter what anyone said to her, her only response was tears. It didn't take long for officers from the county to arrive; they put Yingzhi in the back of their police car.

A few days later Yingzhi finally learned that it was her mother who had saved her from Guiqing, burning herself in the process. Over 70 percent of her body was burned. There was nothing the doctors at the county hospital could do to save her, so Yingzhi's father and brothers rushed her to Hankou. It took all night to transport her there on a cart. They sold off everything of value in the house to pay for her medical bills; they even sold the family ox. But in the end, they couldn't save Yingzhi's mother. When she died, her face was burned black and no one could recognize who she was. But just before she died, she kept mumbling something over and over. Only Yingzhi's father could understand what she was saying: she was calling out her daughter's name, *Yingzhi.*

XVIII

That's how Yingzhi ended up behind bars at the prison. Those flames coming off Guiqing never burned her body, but they scorched her soul. Each moment of every day she felt as if that approaching flame were engulfing her, scorching her, torturing her. Every day she drank glass after glass of cold water in a futile attempt to extinguish that flame. Even though it was cold outside, whenever she washed she would take cold showers. But that flame kept stubbornly burning, refusing to be extinguished.

Yingzhi later became close with her roommate, Sister Yu. Sister Yu had spent a long time on the inside and was good at analyzing the details of various cases. After examining all the aspects of Yingzhi's case, she heaved a deep sigh. Sister Yu told Yingzhi, "I don't see any outcome but the death penalty for this case."

Yingzhi no longer felt sad about that outcome. She just quietly passed the time during her remaining days. On bright clear days she would reflect on the life she once lived, and during those moments she couldn't help but ask herself, *How could all this have happened?*

Yingzhi spent the entire winter in prison waiting for the final judgment to be issued. When the verdict finally came down, she wasn't even in the mood to read it. That's because she knew that no matter what the verdict said, that flame in her heart was already destined to consume her.

Spring came and the wildflowers were in full bloom beside the river. Yingzhi was taken in shackles out to the execution ground. No one from her family came to see her. She knew that her father was plagued by poverty and illness and her brothers were in deep debt. Yingzhi understood that she was responsible for ruining the family. After she was dead, there would be nobody to claim her body; her family had nothing but hatred and disdain for her. Yingzhi thought they were right to hate her.

Kneeling in the dirt, Yingzhi faced the muzzle of the executioner's rifle. The shot rang out and she fell to the ground. The second her head fell to the side, she saw the bed of wildflowers covering the execution ground in all directions. She thought they were just as beautiful as the flowers beside the river in Phoenix Ridge. And then she seemed to see a small child running through that sea of wildflowers. She gently uttered his name: *Jianhuo.*

2001, Wuhan

TRANSLATOR'S AFTERWORD

She knew that if she didn't say her piece, that flame would never be extinguished; even after death, it would continue raging...

Fang Fang, *The Running Flame*

*T*he Running Flame opens with the protagonist, Yingzhi, in prison awaiting her execution. And in those final hours, her last desperate urge is to "say her piece"—or in the original, *bixu shuochu yiqie*, she "must get everything out." The thrust, even necessity, to say it all, to get it all out, is what lies at the heart of the novel. And while some might read this necessity as a form of moral unburdening after having committed an act of murder, in some sense it is more an act of testimony to the violence *she* suffered. Furthermore, although this may be the story of one woman, that testimony, told in the face of erasure and silence, also functions as a form of collective witnessing, attesting to the violence suffered by generations of women. From her early fiction to her controversial 2016 novel *Soft Burial*, which challenged norms about how history can be portrayed in China, up through *Wuhan Diary*, her explosive account of the

2020 COVID-19 lockdown in Wuhan, Fang Fang has consistently used writing as an outlet to provide witness, to provide testimony to different forms of violence and social injustice. While *The Running Flame* seems to employ a more modest fictional canvas, in many ways this is one of her more complex acts of fictional witnessing.

Originally published in Chinese in 2001, *The Running Flame* (*Benpao de huoguang*) is an explosive short novel. It first appeared in the prestigious literary journal *Harvest* in May 2001 and was later published in a single-volume edition in September 2001 by Changjiang Art & Literature Publishing House. In the two decades since its initial release, *The Running Flame* has been republished in eight different editions, many of which have gone through multiple printings in China. The novel was also critically acclaimed, receiving four major awards in China between 2001 and 2003. More recently, *The Running Flame* has been translated into Spanish and German. It has also been widely marketed in China as part of Fang Fang's "Trilogy of Fate," which includes two other short novels that also explore the fate of different women in modern China.

Fueled by its succinct narrative and gripping story, *The Running Flame* doesn't devote a lot of space to exposition of the larger historical and sociological forces at play. In fact, some readers might be reminded of other works touching on similar themes, like Faith McNulty's 1980 nonfiction book *The Burning Bed* or Taiwanese writer Li Ang's 1983 novel *The Butcher's Wife* (*Sha fu*). But this is a novel deeply tied to the long history of gender politics in contemporary China. It is also greatly informed by the economic and social trends unleashed by Deng Xiaoping's reform era policies. In some sense, it is the strange intersection of these two lines that creates the tragedy that plays out in *The Running Flame*. For that reason, it makes sense to provide a bit of general background on these two topics to better understand the broader historical and social context for Fang Fang's novel.

GENDER

While a full discussion of the place of women in twentieth-century Chinese society goes beyond the scope of this afterword, a short overview is in order. Several years after the Revolution of 1911, which brought the Qing dynasty to an end, a new cultural movement began to take form. In 1919, political events allowed that cultural movement to take on new momentum, and it became reframed as the May Fourth Movement. It was against the backdrop of May Fourth that a younger generation of writers, students, scholars, and intellectuals began to critically reflect on the Chinese political system, the Confucian tradition, and even the Chinese language itself. Another central theme of the May Fourth intellectuals was the question of women. For thousands of years, women were routinely the victims of patriarchal power structures, which were reinforced by Confucian orthodoxy. This resulted in women being denied educational opportunities, refused access to many professions, and subjected to practices such as polygamy, arranged marriages, and bound feet. May Fourth marked a significant turning point where women's rights were openly debated. Some participants in the May Fourth Movement began to advocate for greater access to education for women, improved social equality, and female emancipation. Ibsen's play *A Doll's House*, which was translated by Hu Shi and Luo Jialun under the title *Nora* (*Nuo la*) and published in the progressive journal *New Youth* (*Xin qingnian*) in 1918, ignited new debates on women in society. Lu Xun responded with an influential essay, "What Happens When Nora Leaves

Home," that highlighted the rift between the ideals of the movement and the practical shackles that women still faced because of a lack of progressiveness on the part of societal institutions and mainstream thought. While the Republican period did see some changes to the status of women in Chinese society, including the rise of well-known female public figures like Soong Mei-ling, who became a globally influential political figure, the overall state of women remained precarious. Some of the more prominent Chinese women writers of this period like Ding Ling and Xiao Hong not only chronicled the struggles that so many women faced but also, through their own lives, bore testament to the inequalities women were commonly subjected to.

With the establishment of the People's Republic of China in 1949 came a new promise for Chinese women. Shortly after the founding of the new nation came the enactment of the New Marriage Law (*xin hunyin fa*) on May 1, 1950. The New Marriage Law marked a radical departure from earlier marriage laws and proved to be a major step forward for women by banning compulsory marriage and the practice of taking child brides, raising the legal age for marriage (twenty for males, eighteen for females), and ensuring both parties provided consent. In order to educate citizens about these new standards for marriage, a massive publicity machine was mobilized through which films, stage plays, fiction, and comic books were employed to educate the masses about the importance of gender equality and discourage traditional practices that went against the new law. For millions of Chinese, this more progressive phase would be characterized by the famous catchphrase attributed to Mao Zedong: "Women hold up half the sky." While the Mao era undoubtedly saw progress for women on a number of fronts, such as access to education and greater social mobility than in the pre-1949 era, true gender equality proved elusive.

With the dawn of the reform era in 1978, a new page in contemporary Chinese history began. China launched the Four Modernizations, which saw a drive toward modernization in agriculture, industry, defense, and science, and the Opening Up policies saw the nation begin to more rigorously engage with nations around the world. What should have felt like an era of new opportunities for women was marred by policies that exacted new forms of control over women's bodies. Women found aspects of their sexual and biological lives managed by political organs like neighborhood committees and regulations like the One Child Policy (1979–2015), which would dictate decisions for women about contraception, pregnancy, and abortion. As the reform era deepened, a series of new trials would emerge that would further challenge women's overall status in society. As Leta Hong Fincher observed:

> A combination of factors—skyrocketing home prices, a resurgence of traditional gender norms, legal setbacks to married women's property rights, declining labor force participation among women, and the media campaign against "leftover" women—has contributed to the fall in status and material well-being of Chinese women relative to men.[1]

In some ways, these changes can even be seen as regressive, especially in terms of how increased economic power among men has translated into the return of pre-1949 practices that had been largely eradicated during the Mao era. These include the reinforcement of "traditional gender roles" for numerous occupations, the return of prostitution, and the common practice of wealthy men keeping a "second wife" or mistress. The contradictions at play as China modernized at a breakneck pace while simultaneously reintroducing patriarchal and oppressive practices toward women were palpable. Many Chinese writers and filmmakers in the 1980s and 1990s began to highlight these tensions in their work, and the fate of women became a central theme of films like Xie Fei's *The Woman from the Lake of Scented Souls* (*Xianghun nü*) and Zhang Yimou's string of films *Judou*, *The Story of Qiuju* (*Qiuju da guansi*), and *Raise the Red Lantern* (*Da hongdenglong gaogaogua*), and the fiction of writers like Wang Anyi, Zhang Jie, Zhang Kangkang, and even Fang Fang. While many of these stories were set in premodern China (often as an attempt to elude censorship by avoiding open criticism of gender issues present in contemporary society), they were clearly intent on opening up a new space for reflection on the predicaments that many women were facing in contemporary China.

REFORM

Another important part of the backstory in *The Running Flame* is the economic craze that swept China in the early 1990s and continued to gain momentum in the new millennium. In 1992, Deng Xiaoping launched a "southern tour" to Shenzhen, Zhuhai, Guangdong, and Shanghai, where he encouraged further economic growth. Deng's quotes from his southern tour, like "Development is a firm principle" (*fazhan cai shi ying daoli*), became catchphrases for an entire generation, and new government policies would lead to massive development along China's coastal regions, expand the special economic zones, increase manufacturing, and inject a new energy into China's fledgling stock market. The southern tour marked a turning point that took the reform era into a new phase, which would pull China out of the economic lull it faced after the events in Tiananmen Square in 1989. Increasing numbers of government workers and employees of state-owned factories and businesses "jumped into the sea" of entrepreneurism and private business. Slogans like "To get rich is glorious" (*zhifu guangrong*), "Let some people get rich first" (*rang yibufenren xian fuqilai*), and "Look toward the money" (*xiang qian kan*, a pun that played off the old saying "Look toward the future") not only became catchphrases of the day but also encapsulated a widespread spirit of wild west–style speculation, investment, entrepreneurism, and money-driven dreams that swept over the entire nation.

China began to see yearly economic growth rates in the double digits, the skylines of major cities were transformed by massive construction projects, migrant workers flooded from the countryside to urban centers for better-paying jobs, and many citizens saw a dramatic increase in their standard of living and quality of life. But there was also a dark side to this economic boom. Having largely dismantled and undermined organized religions after 1949 (and especially during the period 1966–1976), socialism and top-down political dictates had long assumed the role of providing society's moral compass. Now that socialism was retreating as the official state ideology and replaced by a rampant capitalist fervor, there seemed to be no moral guardrails in place dictating the extent to which individuals could go to get rich. Popular culture was swift to respond: Li Yang, who became famous throughout China for his wildly popular English instructional curriculum Li Yang Crazy English, told his students that the reason to study English can be boiled down to two words: "Make money!"[2] Films like *Shanghai Fever* (*Gu feng*, literally "Stock Market Fever") captured the unrelentingly speculative craze; the novelist Zhu Wen satirized this era with his novella *I Love Dollars* (*Wo ai meiyuan*); and in his book of social criticism *Random Thoughts on 1993* (*Jiusan duanxiang*), writer Liang Xiaosheng described the widespread "madness" as equivalent to the Great Leap Forward and the

Cultural Revolution, only this time political fervor had been replaced by economic fervor.

It is the collision of these two phenomena (gender inequality and the economic craze of the 1990s) that provides the backdrop for many of the tensions that play out in *The Running Flame*. To more fully understand the motivations driving the characters, whether those be Guiqing's gambling addiction or Yingzhi's decision to sell sexual favors for money, it is important to take this crucial historical backdrop into consideration. As Liang Xiaosheng describes it, the world of *The Running Flame* is indeed a world of madness—a time when yesterday's "proletariat" class suddenly found themselves seduced by a new dream of money and materialism. When Yingzhi seeks safe harbor with her parents after being beaten and abused by her husband, her family's reluctance to help is deeply enmeshed in a thousand-year-old tradition that "daughters, once married, are like spilled water." But what *The Running Flame* expresses in a powerful way is the manner in which these two threads—traditional gender inequality and the contemporary craze to make money—intersect in particularly nefarious ways. This leads to new forms of sexual commodification, the revival and economically driven augmentation of long-standing gender inequalities, and the internalization of moral codes that equate sexuality and self-worth with transactional value. While Yingzhi is very much a victim of the patriarchal systems of oppression and violence that have become deeply ingrained within the fabric of mainstream society and social values, she is also a victim of the capitalist forces of consumption and material desire that became the taglines and slogans for her generation. But when the internalization of the latter impulse to attain economic prosperity (in the guise of fancy new clothes, a new house, or simply a wad of cash) can be fulfilled only by using one's own body as sexual capital, it becomes the very mechanism by which the traditional machinery of patriarchal oppression is fueled and expanded.

FICTION

Of course, besides these historical factors playing out behind the scenes, there is also the practical story behind the novel's composition. Although it is a work of fiction, Fang Fang has spoken about the real-life inspiration behind the story. When I asked her about the origin of *The Running Flame*, Fang Fang wrote:

> At the time there was a popular television show in China called *Thirteen Murders* (*Ming'an shisan zong*).[3] I was actually the one who conducted the interviews for that show—I interviewed thirteen different murderers for the program. I spent a lot of time listening to them narrate their stories of how they came to commit these crimes. At the time, I didn't have time to do anything else with those stories. Since I was the editor-in-chief of a magazine, I had to rush back to resume my editorial duties as soon as those interviews were completed. That magazine, which was called *Celebrities Today* (*Jinri mingliu*), was later shut down by the authorities and I found myself with some spare time, so I decided to adapt some of the interview materials into a series of fictional works. *The Running Flame* is one of the works that came out of that; another one was the novella entitled *The Water Follows the Sky* (*Shui sui tian qu*). Both stories are about the fate of Chinese women from the countryside and explore how, over the course of their struggles, these women ended up being forced to commit these crimes.[4]

Directed by Gao Qunshu, *Thirteen Murders* was a sensation when it first aired in 2000. Each episode began with documentary film excerpts from Fang Fang's real-life interviews with women inmates before segueing into the dramatized version that attempted to re-create each story. The television show, alongside Fang Fang's novels from this period, ignited widespread public debate about gender equality, women's rights, human trafficking, and rape and other forms of sexual violence. Episodes five and six of the forty-two-installment series are also inspired by the same real-life story that served as the source material for *The Running Flame*. In the television iteration of the story, Yingzhi (who is referred to as Tong Ling) is actually given a much more sympathetic portrayal. This is done by eliminating her licentious side and completely removing her extramarital affair and flirtatious interactions with members of the song-and-dance troupe. Instead, Tong Ling is portrayed as a more traditional woman of pure heart and values, thus enhancing the audience's sense of identification with her and increasing the sense of tragic victimization when we see her repeatedly raped and beaten by her husband and verbally abused by her in-laws.[5]

In the version of the story told in *The Running Flame*, Fang Fang seems intent on blurring those moral lines. By stripping the lofty and pure moral standing away from Yingzhi, Fang Fang forces us to confront her actions in a new light. Who is the victim? Who is the perpetrator? Who is culpable? What was rendered black and white in *Thirteen Murders* becomes riddled with moral ambiguity and ethical questions in *The Running Flame*. It also becomes an interesting moral exercise for readers of *The Running Flame* to view the version of the story told in *Thirteen Murders* and reflect on how their response to the act of murder may have changed and why.

Of course, between the fictionalized versions of the story told in the television series *Thirteen Murders* and Fang Fang's long-form fictional account told in *The Running Flame*, we should not forget the true story and real lives that inspired these narratives. Both stories borrow heavily from the life of Dong Junhui, a native of the small town of Gangye in Shijia-zhuang, Hebei Province, who was arrested for the murder of her husband, Wu Yanting, in 1999. The act of murder was the climax after Dong had been subjected to more than a decade of rape and abuse at Wu's hands. A few days before the murder, Dong had fled to her parents' house to escape another round of abuse, but her husband followed here there, and on June 21 he threatened to kill her and her entire family. The next day, on the afternoon of June 22, 1999, Wu returned with a container of gasoline in an attempt to burn his in-laws' house down. The following day, June 23, Dong Junhui and her brother managed to tie Wu to a tree in their family courtyard. Dong doused her husband, Wu Yanting, with gasoline and lit him ablaze with a cigarette lighter. Dong and her brother turned themselves over to the local police and were sentenced to death for their roles in the murder. After several rounds of appeal, Dong Junhui's sentence was reduced to life imprisonment before being further reduced to a term that was set from December 4, 2001, to June 3, 2025.

In response to discussions about *The Running Flame*, Fang Fang penned a short essay entitled "How Many Women Like Yingzhi Are Around Us?" ("Women shenghuo Zhong you duoshao Yingzhi?"), which deserves to be quoted at length:

> When it comes to rural women like Yingzhi that appear in my fiction, I often find myself at a loss for words. Sometimes I feel like the simple fact of being born in an impoverished rural area has already decided her tragic fate. Either she silently accepts that fate, living, laboring away her life, and eventually dying there. There she will live a simple and difficult life, completely ignorant

of the outside world. Or she will decide to strive for a new life; but in order to change her fate, she will have to pay an enormous price—sometimes the weight that price carries may prove even heavier than life itself.

Then again, perhaps we are sometimes led askew by generalizations; maybe she will be poor and her life will be difficult, but perhaps she will gain a certain happiness from a life based on hard work? That's how a lot of people see things, especially those rich and entitled urbanites who tend to hold on to that romanticized belief more than others. Of course, we can't say they are wrong; after all, everyone has their own understanding when it comes to this thing called "happiness."

I once heard a friend who had a deep understanding of the Chinese countryside describe it like this: There are swarms of young rural girls flocking into the cities to find work, especially in southern China. Lacking education, life skills, or any practical experience, these girls quickly find themselves without any good options and turn to prostitution. Some of them are forced into it, but the majority go down this route willingly. Once they start making money, they send the vast majority of it home so their parents can build new homes, their younger siblings can go to school, and their elder brothers can get married. But when they get older and return to their hometowns, they quickly find that their parents who are now living in the new house they paid for, their younger siblings who are now in college, and their now married older brothers want nothing to do with them. They are looked at as "dirty"; they are accused of having ruined the family name; they are a shameful stain on the entire family. Whether they are in the city or back home in the countryside, they are always greeted by cold eyes. People see them and only think of them as symbols of decadence and debauchery, but does anyone understand how tragic their lives really are?

Although Yingzhi's path is somewhat different from theirs, she in some sense is still walking in their footsteps. On one level, Yingzhi is a new generation of woman from the countryside. At the very least, she is someone who is not willing to settle for the kind of life she sees around her. She holds on to the belief that a better life awaits her. In fact, she is committed to using her own wherewithal to attempt to build that beautiful new life for herself. But in the end, she fails and it is a tragic failure. You can't assign all the blame for what happened to Yingzhi or her husband or her mother-in-law; she too played a part in what happened.

There is something restless about Yingzhi. She never wanted to study and didn't like working hard. She instead took the easy way to make money. On the one hand, she was flirtatious; but she was also traditional. She didn't know exactly what she wanted, but she knew she wanted something. She was brimming with ambition and yet her heart was filled with cowardice. She was coarse and rash, but there was also something delicate and refined about her. She is the kind of person we can see all around us.

But I don't want to say much more than that. This novel has already expressed everything I wanted to say. Once you read it, you can come to any kind of conclusion you want.[6]

One final conclusion about *The Running Flame* is that while it remains very much a product of its time during the late 1990s, many of its themes remain prescient today. In 2021, celebrity Chinese tennis athlete Peng Shuai disappeared from public view one month after accusing a senior political figure of sexual assault. As the #MeToo movement opened the door to renewed discussions about sexual violence and other gender-based forms of inequality all over the world, in China a major political crackdown on the movement was launched.[7] And then in January 2022, a video of a female victim of human trafficking kept in chains in Jiangsu Province sent Chinese social media ablaze. The following month, a vlogger named Li from Yulin in Shaanxi bragged about keeping his wife locked in an iron cage.[8] Both stories prompted official investigations and a public outcry. But these extreme cases also signaled the deep gender inequalities, violence toward women, and hidden atrocities silently playing out against the backdrop of the "harmonious society" during an "age of prosperity." Though a work of fiction, *The Running Flame* is deeply rooted in the real-life events it is inspired by and, at the same time, functions as a form of collective witnessing for those unable to tell their stories. In her 2000 essay, Fang Fang asked, "How many women like Yingzhi are around us?" Perhaps the greatest tragedy of *The Running Flame* is that more than twenty years after Fang Fang brought this woman's tragic story to life, there remain many Yingzhis still silently suffering among us.

M.B.

August 16, 2023

NOTES

1. Leta Hong Fincher, *Leftover Women: The Resurgence of Gender Inequality in China* (London: Zed Books, 2014), 7.

2. See Li Yang's comments in the documentary film *Crazy English* (*Fengkuang yingyu*), directed by Zhang Yuan (PRC: Xi'an Film Studio, 1999).

3. Fang Fang is credited as one of four screenwriters on the dramatic series *Thirteen Murders*, along with Xu Duoli, Liu Xiaomei, and Li Jingmin. Episodes five and six of the forty-two-installment series are also inspired by the same real-life story that served as the source material for *The Running Flame*.

4. Private correspondence with Fang Fang, May 17, 2023.

5. Private correspondence with Fang Fang, May 17, 2023.

6. "How Many Women like Yingzhi Are Around Us?" ("Women shenghuo Zhong you duoshao Yingzhi?"), originally published in *Dangdai zuojia pinglun* 1 (2002): 118.

7. Huizhong Wu, "China's Crackdown on #MeToo Movement Extends Far Beyond Tennis Star Peng Shuai," *PBS News Hour*, November 24, 2021, https://www.pbs.org/newshour/world/china-crackdown-on-metoo-movement-extends-far-beyond-tennis-star-peng-shuai.

8. For more on these cases, see Aowen Cao and Emily Feng, "The Mystery of the Chained Woman in China," National Public Radio (NPR), February 17, 2022, https://www.npr.org/sections/goatsandsoda/2022/02/17/1080115082/the-mystery-of-the-chained-woman-in-china; and Lars James Hamer, "Live Streams Brags About Locking Wife in Cage," *That's China*, March 3, 2022, https://www.thatsmags.com/china/post/34116/live-streamer-brags-about-locking-his-wife-in-a-cage.

ACKNOWLEDGMENTS

Thanks first to Fang Fang not only for providing literary inspiration but also for being a great model of moral courage. I want to also express my deep thanks to the two external readers who went above and beyond the call of duty with their generous comments, suggestions, and in some cases creative input for alternative wordings for specific passages in the text. My deep appreciation for my agent Jennifer Lyons and the wonderful editorial team at Columbia University Press, including Jennifer Crewe, Christine Dunbar, Krystyna Budd, and Wren Haines. Finally, thanks to all my colleagues, students, friends, and family for their continued support.